T0113823

Babygirl

Prequel to Black Butterfly

Lorna Jackie Wilson

authorHOUSE®

AuthorHouse™
1663 Liberty Drive
Bloomington, IN 47403
www.authorhouse.com
Phone: 1-800-839-8640

© 2014, 2015 Lorna Jackie Wilson. All rights reserved.

No part of this book may be reproduced, stored in a retrieval system, or
transmitted by any means without the written permission of the author.

Published by AuthorHouse   01/08/2015

ISBN: 978-1-4969-3758-2 (sc)
ISBN: 978-1-4969-3757-5 (e)

Library of Congress Control Number: 2014915776

Any people depicted in stock imagery provided by Thinkstock are models,
and such images are being used for illustrative purposes only.
Certain stock imagery © Thinkstock.

This book is printed on acid-free paper.

Because of the dynamic nature of the Internet, any web addresses or links contained in
this book may have changed since publication and may no longer be valid. The views
expressed in this work are solely those of the author and do not necessarily reflect the views
of the publisher, and the publisher hereby disclaims any responsibility for them.

Cover Design: Lorna Jackie Wilson

Contents

Part I: The 70s

Part II: The 80s

Dedication

To my mother, Carrie Wilson Jones (Belle Starr). Carrie Wilson Jones was a very giving woman, especially when it came to helping others. She was fun and loving and had a carefree demeanor. She gave freely from her heart, was passionate about music, and loved to dance. Two of her favorite songs were "Me and Mrs. Jones" and "Lost in a Masquerade." Life on earth was short for my mother. It was difficult for me to accept the circumstances that took her from her children. While it isn't easy to overcome obstacles that impede one's journey, it's not uncommon for those on the path to experience grief or pain, especially with the loss of a loved one.

During rehabilitation, she continually sought to regain custody of her children, even while facing challenges and circumstances beyond her control. Her undying love and commitment was heartfelt. It is without doubt that Carrie Wilson Jones loved her children, and it is with certainty that she was loved by her children and family. We knew her heart, and regardless of circumstance, a child will love his or her mother unconditionally, and I am no exception.

With sincere love and devotion, I dedicate *Babygirl: Prequel to Black Butterfly* to my mother, Carrie Wilson Jones. I love you, Mom.

To my mother, Acie Spraddling, my mother through foster care. Although she is one of my four foster mothers, she impacted my life the most. Not only did she live life by example and introduce me to Father God and His precious Son, Jesus Christ, she also embraced me and helped me overcome issues associated with loss and self-esteem.

Foster care can be a positive, life-changing experience in the right home. I am thankful that God saw fit to place me with such a dynamic woman. Acie Spraddling is blessed with the gift of compassion, and she is committed to helping others. To this day, she continues to provide foster care and support to children; it is her life's work. Her influence was paramount in future decisions I made that led to positive change. With sincere love and devotion, I dedicate *Babygirl: Prequel to Black Butterfly*, to my mother, Acie Spraddling. I love you, Mom.

Acknowledgments

With sincere appreciation, I acknowledge my children, Wanavia, Celeste, Matthew, and Christian. Each child has special significance in my heart.

Wanavia is the diamond that sparked instant redirection in my life. Wanavia is my firstborn child I had when I was a teenager. She is the gift that perpetuated positive change. This pregnancy came about at a time when my mother decided to leave her children for fear of her life and the lives of her children. My siblings and I woke up one morning to find a note indicating she was not going to return and not to look for her. My siblings and I bounced from house to house among several different friends and relatives. Not knowing where to go or where I belonged, I began to long for love and acceptance, and I found myself pregnant at age sixteen. This pregnancy and the circumstances surrounding it led to life-changing decisions and eventual foster care placement with Acie Spraddling.

With sincere appreciation, I acknowledge my daughter, Celeste. Celeste is a social magnet who facilitates family cohesiveness. She is the coordinator of all family events and the life of all events; she generates positive energy that everyone loves. Her bubbly personality motivates those around her to embrace fun, laughter, and love. Her beautiful personality is indicative of her name, which means "heavenly."

With sincere appreciation, I acknowledge my firstborn son, Matthew. Matthew is the articulate analyzer of family situations. He has the foresight to see what could or should be. His gift of assessment provides insight about possibilities that may not have been previously considered. His intuitiveness influences new ideas and reflection. Matthew in Hebrew means "gift of God." The religious meaning of the name is evidenced by the fact it was given to Saint Matthew; according to Christian theology, he was one of Jesus Christ's twelve disciples (Answers 2014).

With sincere appreciation, I acknowledge my son Christian, my miracle baby. During labor, there was no amniotic fluid to give birth. I was in my tenth month of pregnancy when I was told, "There is a problem." With no medication to reduce pain, combined with induced labor, contractions came one right after the other. There was no break in between contractions to rest or recover as with previous pregnancies. However, I would not trade the experience for anything in the world. With great pain, comes great joy. Christian is the kindest, sweetest child; he is my heart.

Of course, all my children are miracles, and I love them dearly. Yet each child has his or her own special gift, and I am blessed and honored to call them my own. I love you, babies.

Foreword

In 1980, the Lord blessed me to become a foster parent to teenage mothers and their babies. At first, I was not sure of this calling because my husband had reservations about the possible challenges teenage foster care might entail. However, after I prayed about it, the Lord made it plain to me in a dream in which a child was on my shoulder, and she was pregnant. Shortly thereafter, Lorna Jackie Wilson came to me, and she was that child.

My lifestyle included church and prayer, so it was important for me to instill values and morals in the characters of the children in my care, and church was a huge part of our lives. I took Lorna to church with me every time I went. Eventually, Lorna gave her life to the Lord, and we became close as mother and daughter. A few months later, she had her first child. After that, she went everywhere I went. I was proud to be her mother and grandmother to her daughter.

Lorna is still in my life; I love her, and I know she loves me. After more than thirty years, we are still close, and she visits me as much as she can. All her children call me Granny.

Lorna Jackie Wilson

From 1980 to today, I continue to provide foster care to children, some with challenges and special needs. Nevertheless, God provides us with whatever we need to conquer challenges and build strong relationships. In this regard, Lorna has developed relationships with many of the foster children I provide care for, and today, they are a huge part of her extended family.

—Acie Spraddling

Preface

In an "ideal" family, the family structure may consist of caring parents, obedient children, and financial stability. However, it's unrealistic to assume every child comes from such a structure as there are numerous factors that shape family structures, including environment, socioeconomic status, ethnicity, faith, and even the law.

When a family is dysfunctional and intervention isn't an option in the biological setting, foster care may be an alternative solution. When properly monitored and supported, foster care can serve as an intervention that supports overall stability. Yet there are other variables to consider with successful intervention.

Although placement in foster care is often the basic form of intervention for seriously maltreated children, youth often need additional services to address their family problems and maltreatment. Understanding the outcomes of placement in out-of-home care requires assessment of the level and type of other services provided. Yet child welfare case records are often incomplete sources of services received because not all services are paid for or provided by the child welfare agency (Pecora et al. 2003, 20). Consequently, findings reveal that it is not uncommon for children to require additional services to mature as productive citizens. This may include academic support as well as implementation of strategies that support positive behavior.

Moreover, the Casey National Alumni Study reveals 69.7 percent of students in foster care complete high school and only 10.8 percent of that number attain bachelor's degrees or higher. (Pecora et al. 2003, exhibit 5.1, 28).

Therefore, there is reason to believe that successful intervention includes a comprehensive approach from a number of different resources, e.g., educators, mentors, counselors, clergy, family members, etc., but a comprehensive approach to intervention is not always affordable or available. Its implementation could nonetheless provide the best support for youth development and educational achievement.

Giving consideration to the Casey National Alumni case study and circumstances that may occur in both biological and foster-care settings, *Babygirl: Prequel to Black Butterfly* was written to share the story of a young girl's journey through the foster care system and its impact on her life.

Introduction

It's 1977, and children are outside, jumping on pavement outlined in white chalk in a hopscotch pattern. A few feet away, two little girls are swinging a jump rope while a third child jumps in the middle. There is laughter as children play and have fun.

On the corner, a man pulls up in a black Cadillac Seville and a young boy approaches the car. The man hands the young boy a small plastic sandwich bag. It's difficult to identify the contents of the bag from a distance. The man drives away; the boy puts the bag in his pocket.

Meanwhile, Catherine is at home cooking dinner for her children, Michelle, Tina, and Leon. The aroma of greens and cornbread fills the house. Catherine walks from the kitchen to the living room and selects an album from her vinyl collection of albums and 45s. She places the album *Breezin'* on the record player, gently drops the needle, and turns up the volume. She lights a cigarette, takes one draw, tilts her head, and sways to the soulful, jazz sounds of George Benson. Life is good.

Tina, Michelle, and Leon smell the aroma of their mother's cooking from outside. "I'm going to get something to eat. That food smells good. I'm hungry," Tina says.

"I'm right behind you," Leon replies.

Michelle laughs. "Me too."

The three go into the house, ready for dinner. "Wash your hands! Don't touch anything until you wash your hands," Catherine yells.

After washing their hands, the children make their plates; each child takes his or her plate to a different room to eat. Once the children are out of sight, Catherine enters the bathroom and opens the medicine cabinet to retrieve several items. She remains in the bathroom for over thirty minutes. Upon exit, she goes in her bedroom, turns on the television, lies on the bed, and falls asleep.

Prologue

Mother Love

Music plays the latest hits. Trails of incense fill the room.
The lava lamp twirls as colors dance and play upon the moon.
Smoke and fragrance intertwine to create a special scent.
Polaroids hang within the net as the record player spins.

Siblings play with paddle ball while another plays with jacks.
Mother plays with sugar hill and fills her arm with smack.
Empty cupboards sing a song for every child to hear.
Grumbling are the hunger pangs standing in the mirror.

Buses run from dusk to dawn. The tickets are for free.
Movies at the Fox Theater. Our favorite is Bruce Lee.
Penny candy at the store. There's plenty to pass around.
The meat market where food is carved and ordered by the pound.

Siblings play with Hula-Hoops while another plays basketball.
Mother faces welfare staff. Then comes the final call.
Hugs bestowed on every child. Kisses placed upon their heads.

Lorna Jackie Wilson

The love is true. The pain is real. Tears are softly shed.

Whisked away into a car, each child a different route.
One heads north, another east, the last one's headed south.
Unfamiliar are surroundings in homes decked out in style.
Keen eyes assess appearance of every single child.

Clothing dull and tattered. They're led on a shopping spree.
Allowance for new wardrobe. Stacy Adams on their feet.
Longing for mother's love, for this was always true.
If only to see her one more time and kiss and hug her too.

Cast

1. Catherine Hilton
2. Grace Hilton (Catherine's mother)
3. Tina Hilton (Catherine's daughter)
4. Michelle Hilton (Catherine's daughter)
5. Leon Hilton (Catherine's son)
6. Phil Hilton (Catherine's brother)
7. Mike Hilton (Catherine's brother)
8. Jessie Hilton (Catherine's brother)
9. Stacy Hilton (Catherine's little sister who is ten, twenty-two years younger than Catherine)
10. Felicia Preston (Catherine's best friend)
11. Victor Sinclair (aka Vic, Catherine's boyfriend)
12. Tony Lord (owner of Club Karaoke)

Supporting Cast

1. Chauncey (Tony's assistant)
2. Gary (Tina's boyfriend)
3. Cedric (Michelle's friend)
4. Asia (student 1)
5. Pat (student 2)
6. Rachel (student 3)
7. Mr. Ford (principal)
8. Ms. Williams (teacher)
9. Ms. Fuller (school receptionist)
10. Ms. Saunders (caseworker)
11. Ms. Dayton (youth home director)
12. Judge Balton
13. Attorney Bill Michaels
14. Dr. Collins
15. Kevin and Emma Johnson (foster parents 1)
16. Jessica—Kevin and Emma's daughter
17. Lillie Harvard (foster parent 2)
18. Trent (Victor's friend)
19. Gloria (Trent's girlfriend)
20. Darnell (Victor's runner)

Part I: The 70s

Chapter One

School Days

It's 1977. It's 6:00 a.m., and the clouds are heavy with rain. The home where Michelle and her siblings live is in Detroit. Michelle's mother, Catherine, is sleeping soundly when the alarm startles her. It's a school day; it's time to wake the children. She stretches her arms and yawns. She rubs her eyes and walks toward Tina's room. Tina is Catherine's eldest child. When Catherine arrives at the door, she opens it without knocking.

"Tina, get up. Wake up your brother and get ready for school."

Tina turns her body in the opposite direction and returns to sleep.

"Tina," Catherine repeats. "I said get up. It's time to get ready for school."

Tina positions her legs across the edge of the bed, stretched her arms to the ceiling, and says, "Okay, Mom. I hear you. I'm getting up. Give me a minute, okay?"

Tina walks to the bathroom and prepares to shower. As she turns on the water, she hears a gurgling sound through the pipes and the water runs yellow. Tina waits for it to clear, cleans out the tub, and steps into the shower. As the water streams down to her face, she thinks about school that day and the girl who constantly picks on her. Today she plans to stand up for herself. Tina grabs a towel to dry off and get dressed. She goes to her sister's room.

"Michelle, you need to get up and take your shower now, and don't forget to brush your teeth. Oh, and wake up your brother." Tina is like a second mom.

Michelle yawns and replies, "You're talking too loud. Dang. I just woke up."

Michelle walks across the room and knocks on Leon's door. "Leon, it's time to get up. We have to hurry up and get ready for school. The bus leaves at seven-oh-five."

Michelle grabs her curling iron and heads for the bathroom. Leon jumps out of the bed and rushes for the bathroom. Knocking on the door loudly, Leon says, "Hey, you gotta hurry up and come out of there. I have to go. I need to use it now."

Michelle replies, "I just got in here, but alright, hurry up. You know it takes me a while to curl my hair."

As the siblings get ready for school, Catherine yells, "It's six-thirty, people. You know when that bus leaves. You better hurry up and get to the bus stop. Miss the bus and you walk. But you're getting out of here."

Tina says, "Okay we're leaving. Just trying to finish a quick bowl of cereal. Did you eat, Michelle?"

"Yes, just can't get these wrinkles out of my clothes," Michelle replies.

Tina says, "Move out of the way. Let me iron it for you. We have to go."

Tina irons Michelle's blue jeans and blouse and passes them to her. "Okay, now get dressed."

Tina, Michelle and Leon leave their home at 6:50 a.m. and walk fast to the bus stop two blocks away. Leon peers down the street and says, "I think I see the bus coming. Y'all better run."

The three siblings run for the bus and make it just in time. The bus doors open, they step onto the bus, and they pay their fares. They look for places to sit, but the bus is crowded, so they have to stand and hold on to the top rail for support. When the bus brakes suddenly at the next stop, the students sway toward one another. They have to hold the rail more tightly to maintain their balance.

Finally, they arrive at school. Tina, Leon, and Michelle wave to one another as they go to their classrooms.

As Tina walks to her desk, Asia throws a square pencil eraser at her head and laughs. When the eraser hits Tina, everyone in the class laughs. Today is not the day. Tina walks across the room and says, "You think that shit is funny. I'm sick of you."

Tina slaps Asia in the face, and they begin to fight. Ms. Williams, the teacher, yells, "Break it up. Break it up now!"

Tina and Asia continue to fight. Ms. Williams calls for security. As the fight continues, other students surround the girls while laughing and rooting for the person they want to win.

At last, security arrives and pulls the girls apart. They are both sent to the principal's office.

Mr. Ford, the principal, is sitting behind his desk. Security has already radioed ahead to alert him that the girls are being escorted to his office. When they arrive, he taps his pencil several times on his desk. "What's going on, ladies? What's the problem?"

Tina replies, "Asia has been bothering me ever since school started this year, and I'm tired of it. I'm not taking it anymore."

"Is this true, Asia? Are you bothering Tina?"

Asia replies, "She thinks she's better than everybody else. Always trying to tell people what to do. I'm sick of her."

Mr. Ford replies, "Well, ladies, I'm going to have to call your parents. You're both suspended pending parent/teacher conferences."

Tina replies, "Oh no, Mr. Ford, please don't call my mother. She's going to kill me if you suspend me. Can't you just give me detention or something?"

"Tina, given the state of your faces, I can't simply brush this off with a warning. You have blood on your clothes. Both of you have to go home."

Asia says, "Dumb bitch. It was just an eraser, but you had to blow it out of proportion."

Tina says, "Call me bitch again and I'll bash your face in some more."

"Do I need to call security back in here? Get it together and learn how to carry yourselves as young ladies, understood?" Mr. Ford asks.

Tina and Asia reply, "Yes sir."

Mr. Ford calls Catherine, Tina's mother, but there is no answer. He leaves a voicemail message and wrote referral letters for both Tina and Asia to take home to their parents. Tina knows she has to get home and erase the voicemail message before her mother plays it back.

The Voicemail

Tina leaves school and heads to the bus stop; she's anxious to get home to erase the voicemail message. She gets on the bus and ponders how she will pretend to go to school for the next week while on suspension without her mother finding out. She must think of a plan. As for the parent/teacher conference, she will cross that bridge when she gets to it.

Tina steps off the bus, places her key in the door, and walks inside. She rushes to the answering machine and listens through the messages. She deletes Mr. Ford's message and breathes a sigh of relief.

In the meantime, Catherine is still in her bed asleep. Tina quietly goes into the kitchen and washes the dishes and sweeps the floor. She looks around the house, checking to see what else needs to be done that will put her mother in a great mood when she awakes. She looks at the clock. It is only 10:25 a.m. School doesn't let out until 3:00 p.m. She would just tell her mom that her menstrual cycle has come and she had to leave because she didn't have sanitary napkins. *Yes*, Tina thinks, *that will work.*

It is third hour; Michelle is in class when the bell rings. While going to her locker to get her textbook for the next class, a student taps her on the shoulder.

"Michelle, did you hear what happened?"

"No. What's up?"

"Your sister got into a fight with Asia. I heard they were suspended."

"What? Where's Tina now?"

"I think she went home."

"I've got to go. Wait until I tell Leon."

Michelle went to the office and asks to have her brother paged. The receptionist replies, "Michelle, why do you want to have your brother paged? He's in class. Is it important?"

"Yes, I have a very important message I have to give him from our mother."

The receptionist replies, "Just give it to me and I'll make sure he gets it."

"No, I can't do that," Michelle says. "It's private."

"Okay, Michelle, I'll page him for you."

When Leon arrives at the office, Michelle tells him what she had heard about Tina. The two leave the building and head to the bus stop.

The Plan

Michelle and Leon arrive home. Tina hears the key click in the cylinder and quickly opens the door to quiet them before they can speak. Tina whispers, "What are y'all doing here?"

"We heard you had a fight with Asia, so we left," Michelle says.

"Where's Asia now? I don't hit girls, but I know someone I can get to whip her ass for you. Do you want me to call her?" Leon asks.

"No," Tina says. "I need y'all to leave before you wake up Momma. She can't know I was suspended. Y'all are messing up my plan."

Leon replies, "We're trying to help you out. But okay, no problem, I'm out." Leon leaves, and the door makes a thud upon his exit. Catherine rises and yells from her room, "What the hell is going on? Who's in here?"

Tina replies, "It's just me, Mom. I'm sick."

Tina whispers to Michelle, "Go hide in your room quickly before she comes in here." Michelle retreats to her room and hides under the bed.

Catherine enters the living room. "Tina, what do you mean you're sick? You were fine this morning."

Tina replies, "I started my cycle, Mom, and then I started cramping too. But I didn't want to disturb you. Sorry if I woke you."

"I was about to get up anyway. Do you need some aspirin or something?"

Tina replies, "I have some, Mom. Thanks. I think I'm going to lie down for a while." Tina walks toward her bedroom, looks around to make sure her mother is out of sight, and heads to Michelle's room.

The Deceit

"Michelle, where are you?" Tina asks in a whisper.

"Under the bed," Michelle answers.

"Okay, you can leave now. Do you know somewhere you can go until school lets out?"

"No. Mostly everyone I know is in school."

"Okay, well, here. Take this money and go see a movie. Make sure you're home within thirty minutes after school dismisses."

"Alright, thanks."

The Referral—One Week Later

It's a Friday afternoon, and Mr. Ford begins to call parents scheduled for parent/teacher conferences. He stops at Tina's referral and remembers there was no answer the first time he called. Therefore, he dials the number, hoping to catch Catherine at home.

The Call

A wall-mounted telephone rings in Catherine's kitchen. On the third ring, Catherine picks up the telephone. "Hello, Catherine speaking. Who's calling?"

"This is Mr. Ford, principal of Remus Robinson Middle School. I'm calling to speak with the parent or guardian of Tina Hilton."

"This is she."

"Ms. Hilton, Tina was suspended last week for fighting. I called and left a message on your voicemail, and I also sent a referral note home by Tina."

"Oh, really? I never received a voicemail or a referral."

Mr. Ford responds, "Hmm, that's odd. In either case, the meeting is next Monday at 9:00 a.m. in my office. Will you be able to make it?"

Catherine says, "Yes, I'll be there. Thank you." Catherine hangs up. She is fuming.

The Fury

Tina and her siblings arrive home. They're laughing and happy to be home from school. "Michelle, girl, I'm so tired. I'm glad it's Friday. It's the weekend, and I'm going out tonight."

Michelle replies, "I wish I was old enough to go out by myself, but I have to be in when the street lights come on. That's so wrong."

Leon says, "Yeah, that sucks. Well, see ya. Wouldn't want to be ya." Leon laughs and walks down the street.

Tina yells, "Leon aren't you going to come in and get something to eat before you leave?"

"Nah, I'm straight. Y'all go ahead."

Tina and Michelle walk in the house. Catherine is sitting on the sofa, smoking a cigarette. Addressing Tina, Catherine asks, "How was school today?"

Tina replies, "It was fine. I'm glad it's Friday. I'm about to grab and quick bite and go out with my friends, okay?"

"I don't think so, Tina. I just got off the phone with Mr. Ford. You must think I'm stupid or something. Get your ass in your room. You're not going anywhere tonight."

Tina replies, "Oh yes, I am. I've been planning to go out with my friends all week, and I'm going."

"Step out that door and it'll be your last time, Tina, and I mean that. Test me if you want to. I will beat the black off of you."

Tina goes to her room and slams the door. Two hours later, she slips out the bedroom window and heads to the bus stop.

It's about 2:00 in the morning before Tina returns home. She gently places her door key in the cylinder in an attempt to sneak back into the house. Catherine is sitting on the sofa waiting for her. There is a belt draped across her lap.

The Meeting

It's 6:00 Monday morning. Catherine is preparing for her meeting with Mr. Ford. She showers and selects an outfit to wear.

"Tina, you know we have that meeting this morning with Mr. Ford. Wake up your brother and sister for school and start breakfast."

Tina wakes up Michelle and Leon. She walks to the kitchen to find something quick to eat. "Looks like we'll be having pop tarts and milk this morning, Mom."

"That's good enough. They'll have lunch in school," Catherine says.

As everyone prepares to leave, they cut off the lights, lock the door, and head for the bus stop. Thirty minutes later, they walk into school.

"Okay, Michelle and Leon, go to class. Where's the office, Tina?"

Tina leads the way.

Catherine and Michelle walk into the office. Ms. Fuller, the receptionist, is sitting behind a desk, typing.

"Excuse me. Good morning ma'am. We have a nine o'clock appointment with Mr. Ford. My name is Catherine Hilton, and this is my daughter, Tina Hilton."

"One moment please, while I get Mr. Ford on the line." Ms. Fuller dials the extension to Mr. Ford's office. He picks up.

"Yes, Ms. Fuller?"

"Mr. Ford, Ms. Hilton and her daughter, Tina, are here for their appointment."

"Send them in."

Catherine and Tina enter Mr. Ford's office.

"Good morning. Please have a seat, Ms. Hilton and Tina."

Catherine and Tina sit.

"Thank you for coming, Ms. Hilton."

"You're welcome. I just wish it could have been on better terms."

"Yes, so do I. As you may know, there's only one week of school left before summer vacation. I sincerely hope Tina and Asia can resolve their differences and return to school in the fall without long-term suspensions."

"Most definitely, Mr. Ford. You will not have any more problems with Tina. Right, Tina?"

"Yes ma'am."

"Well with that being said, let's not go into all of the details surrounding the fight. We know students are going to have disagreements. We just need to guide them toward better choices with conflict resolution. Tina, if you have any issues with Asia in the future, please talk to an administrator, teacher, or security personnel. Please do not take matters into your own hands, understood?"

"Yes sir."

"Alright, you may return in the fall provided you have no more issues with Asia for the remainder of the school year. Again, there's only one week left. Hopefully, Asia and you are able to conduct yourselves as young ladies from this point forward."

"Oh, she will, Mr. Ford, she will. Thank you. I appreciate your leniency in this matter."

"Alright. Have a good day, Ms. Hilton, and you too, Tina."

"Thanks, Mr. Ford," Tina says.

The last week of school arrives, and there have been no further incidents between Tina and Asia. It is summer vacation.

Chapter Two

The Friendship

Catherine sends the children to their grandmother's house and tells them to stay with her for a few days until her food stamps come in. After they leave, she showers and searches her closet for an outfit to wear before her boyfriend arrives to pick her up that night. She selects a brown leather jacket with matching leather pants and places them on her bed. She looks in the mirror at her hair and notices that her finger waves are frizzy. She calls her friend Felicia.

"Felicia, please come over here and do my hair. I'm leaving in an hour or two and need you to hook me up."

"Girl, where you going? I want to go," Felicia says.

"I'm going out with my man tonight, but guess what? I gotta little something for you, but you have to hook me up first."

"I'll be right over."

Felicia arrives in twenty minutes and begins to wash, gel, and rewave Catherine's hair. They laugh and talk about their boyfriends. Meanwhile, the television is running an episode of *Good Times*, and Catherine turns up the television just in time to hear the character of James Evans Jr. say, "I'm kid dy-no-mite." Catherine and Felicia laugh. "He's so hilarious. Now I see why the kids watch this so much."

Felicia finishes Catherine's hair, and they retreat to the bathroom. Catherine pulls a syringe from her purse and a small rubber hose.

Going Out Tonight

Felicia walks toward the door and yells, "Well, lady, let me get out here and find me some business of my own. See you later, okay?"

"Thanks, Felicia. I'll call you next weekend."

Felicia leaves the house. Catherine returns to her bedroom and puts on her brown leather outfit, which fits her like a second skin. At age thirty-two, Catherine is a very beautiful woman. She prides herself on keeping in shape and staying fit. She has an hour glass figure. She looks at herself in the mirror and sprays a little perfume on her neck and wrists.

Thirty minutes later, the doorbell rings. It's her boyfriend, Victor. Catherine opens the door. "Hey baby. It's about time you got here."

Victor replies, "Just got off work. Need to jump in the shower right quick. You look nice."

"Thank you, baby. Where are we going tonight?"

"I have this little club in mind, but the cover charge is five dollars per person. You got some money?"

"I have a little bit. I was saving mine for drinks. You can't pay the cover charge?"

"Yeah, I got it. Just want to make sure you gotta little something to. By the way, Trent and Gloria are supposed to be joining us at the club."

"Oh, really? I haven't seen Gloria in a while."

"I know, nor Trent. It's about time we catch up on old times."

"Yes, sounds like fun."

"I told ya I had a little something in mind, tonight. Okay, let me jump in the shower."

Victor showers and comes out of the bathroom with a towel around him. He enters Catherine's bedroom and closes the door. "Come here, baby."

Catherine approaches him, and he attempts to grab her around the waist and pull her close to him. She jumps back. "Vic! Oh no! I just got my hair done, and there's no way I'm going to let you mess up my hair before we go to the club. You better get dressed so we can go. Remember, our friends are joining us. We don't want to be late."

Victor laughs. "Okay, you're right. I'll be ready in a minute."

The Dance

Catherine and Victor arrive at the club. Their friends Trent and Gloria are already there. When Trent sees them, he motions for them to join him at their table.

Catherine and Victor walk up to them, and the women hug while the men face one another, bump shoulders and shake hands in a familiar, nontraditional fashion. Catherine and Gloria look at them and then turn to one another, shake their heads and laugh.

"Sit down, man," Trent says. "Good to see you, chief."

"You got it," replies Victor.

The four sit, talk, laugh and catch up on old times.

Meanwhile, the music is jumping. The DJ drops the needle on "Brick House" by the Commodores. Catherine jumps up. "That's my song. Come on, baby. Come dance with me."

Addressing Trent, Victor says, "Man, let me get up and dance with this woman or I'll never hear the end of it." He laughs and joins Catherine on the dance floor. Catherine sways her hips, throws her head back, and laughs.

Victor and Catherine are dancing and enjoying themselves when suddenly a stranger walks over and tries to cut in on the dance. Victor says, "Excuse me, partner. Step off."

The stranger replies, "It just a dance. Lighten up." The stranger does not leave and attempts to dance with Catherine.

"I said step off."

Catherine appears oblivious to the exchange and continues to dance and have a good time. Victor grabs her abruptly. "Catherine, let's go."

"What's wrong with you?" Catherine asks.

"I said let's go." They return to their table to retrieve their coats.

"Trent, man, I have to go before I hurt somebody. I'll catch you later, alright?"

"Sure, no problem. See you later, man."

Catherine waves good-bye to Gloria. "See you later, Gloria."

"Okay, see you later, Catherine."

The Silence

On the drive home from the club, there is an uncomfortable silence between Catherine and Victor. They do not exchange one word for the entire ride home. Upon entering her house, Victor throws his coat on the sofa and starts yelling at Catherine. "What the hell were you thinking? When you heard me tell that guy to step off, why'd you continue dancing? Were you trying to dance with him?"

"No I wasn't. I was just trying to have a good time. I don't see what the big deal is."

"Oh you don't see what the big deal is." Victor slaps Catherine across the face. "Do you see what the big deal is now?"

Tears well up in Catherine's eyes. "What the hell is wrong with you? I didn't do anything wrong."

"Where's the blow?"

"In the bathroom in the medicine cabinet."

Victor retreats to the bathroom, and Catherine locks herself in her bedroom.

The Bedroom

Twenty minutes later, Victor exits the bathroom and heads for Catherine's bedroom. When he arrives at the bedroom door, he turns the handle, but the door is locked.

"Catherine, open this door. Open this door now!"

"Go home, Vic. I don't want to be bothered with you anymore tonight."

"Oh you don't want to be bothered. Okay. Okay."

Victor bursts through door, breaking the lock. Catherine screams, knowing all too well what is going to happen next.

Chapter Three

Grandma's House

Michelle, Tina, and Leon are sitting at the table to an enormous spread of their grandmother Grace's cooking. Greens, cornbread, macaroni and cheese, fried chicken, and sweet potato pie are spread out on the table. Grace makes the plates and lets everyone know it's time for dinner. Michelle takes a seat, picks up a fork, and digs in.

"This is delicious," Michelle says. "I wish I could take some of this home to Momma."

"No sirree," replies Michelle's Uncle Phil. "There isn't enough for all of us. Hell, it's barely enough for y'all. Now the rest of us have to take smaller portions."

Leon replies, "Y'all greedy anyway. Need to learn how to share."

Tina laughs.

"Alright, you all settle down now and eat. There's enough for everyone," Grace says.

Tina looks up from her plate and observes the state of Michelle's hair.

"Michelle when you get finished eating, you need to go pick up a hot comb and do something to your hair."

"I know what I need to do. Why are you trying to put my business on front street?" Michelle asks.

"It's already on front street. We aren't blind."

Everyone laughs.

"Whatever."

Michelle finishes her dinner and walks to the bathroom to press and curl her hair. Her ten-year-old aunt Stacy peers through the door. "Hey, when you finish, let's go outside and play hopscotch," Stacy says.

Michelle replies, "Okay, I have my jacks too. Nah, I know you don't want to play jacks because you know you're going to lose."

"What? What are you talking about? You can't beat me."

"We shall see."

The girls laugh.

Leon finishes his dinner and leaves the table. As he passes his uncle Phil, he says, "You got some trees on you, Uncle Phil?"

"Yeah, meet me outside."

Phil and Leon go outside, get in a car, turn up the radio, and smoke marijuana.

Tina and Stacy go outside to play hopscotch on the sidewalk. When they finish with hopscotch, they play jacks, and Stacy wins.

"Um, what you say, Michelle. I can't beat who?"

Michelle laughs. "You got lucky."

The girls continue to play and have fun.

The Fight

Victor exits the bedroom, walks to the sofa, and picks up his coat. He leaves the house, slamming the door. The sound brings relief to Catherine as she looks in the mirror and assesses the bruises on her face. She walks into the kitchen, opens the freezer, and retrieves some ice. She puts the ice in a washcloth and places it on her face. After thirty minutes of nursing her wounds, she calls her mother.

The telephone rings three times, and Grace picks up.

"Hi Mom, is Phil there?"

"Hi Catherine. Hold on. Tina, did you see where Phil went?"

"Yes, he and Leon went outside."

"Go get him and tell him to come get this phone."

"Alright."

Tina walks to Phil's car and knocks on the window. When Phil lowers the window, smoke floats from the top. Tina waves it away and says, "Uncle Phil, telephone."

Phil walks into the house, and Grace passes him the phone. Catherine tells Phil what happened.

"He did what? Where's that punk now?" Phil asks.

"He just left."

"Where does he live?"

"If I tell you, promise me you won't kill him. Just teach him a lesson, okay?"

"Okay. What's the address?"

Catherine gives Phil the address. He hangs up the phone and walks outside. As he gets in his car, Phil says, "Leon, that punk Vic just jumped on your mother."

"What?" Leon asks.

"You heard correctly, and now it's time for me and my brothers to go whip his ass. You stay here. I don't want you to have to deal with him one-on-one when you go back home. So I'm not going to involve you. In fact, let me go back in the house for a second and call my brothers. Leon, you need to get out of the car because I'm about to leave."

Leon gets out of the car.

Phil calls his brothers, Mike and Jessie. After sharing with them what happened to Catherine, he gives them Victor's address and asks them to meet him there. He leaves the house, gets in his car, and burns rubber down the street, anxious to get to Victor's house.

When he arrives, he parks half a block away from the house to wait for his brothers. When they pull up, he gets out of his car and walks over to theirs. Mike opens the door, and Phil gets in.

"Okay, listen, Mike and Jessie. Victor may recognize me because I check in on Catherine from time to time. So Jessie, I need you to knock on Vic's door. We'll wait on the other side of the door, out of eyesight, until he comes out. As soon as we see him, we're all going to rush in on him at the same time. Got it?"

In unison, the brothers say, "Got it."

Just then an idea pops into Jessie's head. "You know what, I have the perfect plan. I'm going to pretend like I'm the repo man. That will get him to come out." Jessie says. "No man's going to stay in the house and watch his car get towed away."

"But we don't have a tow truck," Mike says.

"He doesn't know that."

Jessie knocks on the door. Because of Victor's lifestyle, he is very cautious and looks out of the peephole. He does not recognize Jessie. "Who is it?"

Jessie yells, "Sir, I'm with auto repossessions. Normally, I don't knock on doors. I just tow your car. However, it doesn't seem like you're that far behind in payments. So maybe we can work something out."

Victor is furious and immediately opens the door.

"What do you mean? I'm not behind—"

Before Victor can finish his sentence, the brothers rush him.

The Game

Due to the beating placed upon Victor by Phil, Mike, and Jessie, Victor is lying on the floor unconscious. They look at Victor one last time.

"He'll live," Phil says. "Man, I'm hungry. Let's get something to eat."

They leave Victor's house.

"What y'all doing tonight anyway? Let's get some beer and play some cards," Mike says.

"Sounds like a plan. Let's do it," Phil responds.

The three brothers meet up at Jessie's house with beer and pizza. Phil pulls out a deck of cards. The game is Spades. As they play cards, they reminisce over the songs they love to sing together as a group. The brothers are talented, and their combined voices blend tenor, alto, and contralto in harmonious rhythm and sound.

"You know what, Phil? We need to drive down to Hitsville, USA and stand out there and sing as a group until one of the producers comes out to check us out. I know we have the pipes. We just haven't been discovered yet. What do you say?" Mike asks.

"Well, I don't know, Mike. We all have to work. What do you think, Jessie?"

"Maybe we can plan to take off one day or go on a Saturday if they're open."

"Okay, let's plan to go one day next week," Mike says.

"Well, we need to rehearse first. What do you suggest we sing to get their attention?" Phil asks.

Jessie thinks for a minute. "We need to prepare more than one song. Let's do at least three and just keep singing for an hour or two. Plus, we need to rehearse this weekend to prepare for next week's performance."

The brothers nod in agreement and synchronize their schedules for rehearsal.

When the weekend arrives, the brothers rehearse "I Heard it through the Grapevine" by Marvin Gaye and "Cloud Nine" and "I Wish it Would Rain" by the Temptations.

Hitsville, USA the Following Week

On Thursday of the following week, Phil, Mike, and Jessie get up early to arrive at Hitsville, USA as soon as the doors open. They arrive, exit their vehicles, and warm up their voices. Once the harmony is perfect, they begin to sing the songs they have rehearsed. Their voices blend well, and their sound is soulful with pitch-perfect harmony.

A car pulls up, and a group of men gets out to perform on the street as well. It appears they have the same plan. Soon, a female group arrives.

"Wow, they're raining on our parade. How will we be discovered with all this competition?" Jessie asks.

"I guess it's going to take more than one performance to get noticed. Let's not get discouraged. Let's just do our best, and if we're not discovered today, we'll come back. Agreed?" Phil asks.

The brothers agree. They continue to sing for about an hour. When they leave, they are pleased with their efforts in spite of the fact the producers do not seem to have noticed them. They plan to return again the following week.

Chapter Four

Going Home

A few days later, Catherine calls Grace to let her know the kids can return home. Since she has received her check and food stamps, all is well again. Tina, Michelle, and Leon wave good-bye to Grace as they head for the bus stop and looking forward to the comfort of their own beds.

When they arrive home, Catherine is waiting for them. She opens the door with arms stretched wide. The children are glad to see their mother, and she is glad to see them. The bruises on Catherine's face are almost gone, and what little scarring remains she covered with makeup.

"How are my babies? I missed the three of you so much."

"We missed you too, Mom," Michelle says.

"My babies are home. Alright, Tina, there's food in the refrigerator, and since you're the eldest, I want you to cook dinner today. You can cook whatever you want."

"For real? Okay, cool." Tina opens the refrigerator and smiles as it is stocked to capacity. "Yes, now what am I going to make? Hmmm. I know what I'll make. Spaghetti. Michelle, come in here and help me."

"What do you want me to do?" Michelle asks.

"I want you to chop up the onions, garlic, and bell pepper."

"Okay."

"Be careful. Don't cut yourself. You do remember how I showed you how to dice, right?"

"Yes, I remember, Tina. I know what I'm doing."

Tina laughs. "Okay."

After Michelle finishes dicing up a few of the ingredients, Tina adds them to the ground beef along with oregano and seasoned salt and pepper. She turns the beef as it browns. In a separate pot, she prepares the spaghetti sauce. The aromas of garlic, oregano and onions assail their nostrils. "Umm, this is smelling good already," Tina says.

After dinner is ready, Tina prepares the plates and calls everyone for dinner. When they attempt to take their plates to their separate rooms, Catherine says, "No. We are not doing that anymore. From now on, everyone eats at the dinner table like a normal family, understood?"

The children reply, "Yes ma'am."

After dinner, there are dirty dishes everywhere and spaghetti sauce all over the counters and stove.

"Michelle, please go wash the dishes," Tina says. "I cooked, so you know I'm not cleaning up this mess, right?"

"Why can't Leon do anything?" Michelle asks.

Leon replies, "Because I'm a boy. I don't do dishes."

"That is so not fair," Michelle says.

Michelle washes the dishes, and feeling exhausted, she goes to the living room to relax on the sofa and watch television. Fifteen minutes later, Leon is calling her name. When she gets up and walks into the kitchen, she notices that Leon is holding some kind of metal contraption.

"Leon, what do you want?"

"Michelle, grab the other end of this. I'm trying to stretch it so that I can put in the wheel spokes of my bike."

"Oh, okay." Michelle grabs the metal contraption, not realizing it was scorching hot. She screams at the top of her lungs.

Catherine runs out of her bedroom. "What the hell is going on? What's wrong?" Catherine looks at Michelle's hand; the skin is terribly burned. She looks at Leon. "What did you do to her?"

"I was just playing. I didn't know she was going to grab it for real. I put the metal from the window shade in the fire as a joke. I didn't know she would really grab it."

"Have you lost your mind? I'm going to tear your ass up, Leon. Tina, call nine-one-one. Michelle, put your hand in cool water until the ambulance arrives."

Tina calls 911, and the ambulance arrives shortly thereafter. They put Michelle in the ambulance and drive to the nearest hospital. After the doctor attends to Michelle's wounds, he calls for a social worker to investigate the circumstances surrounding the injury. Michelle assures them it was an accident, but they call Child Care Protective Services nonetheless.

The Caseworker

A week later, a Child Care Protective Services caseworker knocks on Catherine's door. Her name is Ms. Saunders, and she has conducted a thorough investigation of the case that involves Michelle, including a background check on Catherine, Tina, Leon, and Victor.

"Who is it?" Catherine asks.

"Child Care Protective Services."

Catherine opens the door. "May I help you?"

"Yes ma'am. My name is Ms. Saunders, and I'm the caseworker assigned to investigate the circumstances surrounding Michelle's most recent visit to the hospital. May I come in?"

"Yes, please come in. Have a seat. Let me assure you that this was an accident, and it'll never happen again. Would you care for a glass of water?"

Ms. Saunders takes a seat on the sofa. "No thank you. Is it possible for you to explain to me how Michelle got those burns?"

"Yes, you see, her brother, Leon, was planning to put some type of metal contraption in his bicycle spoke and left it on the stove by mistake. Michele didn't know it was hot and went to move it since it didn't belong on the stove. It was truly an accident." Catherine is lying.

"I see. Well, I'm making a note of this. With something like this, we have to follow up, especially since Michelle is only eleven. Hopefully, nothing like this will ever happen again."

"I definitely understand how serious this matter is. You can be sure that it will not happen again."

"Alright, well, that's all for now. We'll be in touch. Have a good day."

"Have a good day." Catherine escorts Ms. Saunders to the door and closes it behind her. She walks across the room and enters the bathroom. She exits approximately thirty minutes later and decides to watch television in the living room. She turns the channel and comes across an episode of *Sanford and Son*. Michelle walks in with bandages on her hand.

"What are you watching, Mom?"

"Sanford and Son. I love this show. You go on now. Go outside and play."

"Mom, I can't play with my hand like this."

"Oh yeah, right. Well, go do something."

Michelle leaves, and Leon quietly calls her name while motioning, using his index finger, for her to come to where he is.

"What do you want?" Michelle asks. She is still upset with him for what he had done to her.

"You know I'm sorry. I didn't know you were going to grab it. I was just playing with you."

"Umm, hmmm, okay. What do you want?"

"Listen, you want to go to the movies with me? The new Bruce Lee flick is out."

"I don't have any money."

"Me neither."

"So how can we go to the movies with no money, silly?"

"Tina has money. She's always bragging about how much her boyfriend gives her."

"She's not going to give it to us."

"She might if you ask. Play the sympathy card. Tell her your hand is injured and whatnot and you can't play outside."

"Okay. Okay. I'll ask her."

Michelle takes Leon's advice on how to get money from Tina. It works, and they head to the bus stop. Forty-five minutes later, they arrive at the Fox Theater. *Enter the Dragon* is on the marquee in big letters and bright lights.

Back at home, the telephone rings. Catherine picks up the phone.

"Hey, baby. It's Vic. How ya doing?"

Catherine hangs up.

He dials her again, and Catherine hangs up again.

She calls her friend Felicia for advice.

"Hey, Felicia. What's up, girl? It's been a minute since we talked."

"Yes it has. How are you?"

"I'm alright. I broke up with Vic, and he keeps calling, trying to get back with me. But I'm not going to allow any man to keep hitting on me. Enough is enough."

"I know that's right," Felicia says.

"Felicia, it's just that I'm so lonely. Sometimes I feel like giving in. I'm just not sure if I should give him another chance. I mean if he promises not to hit me again, maybe? What do you think?"

"Do you love him?"

"I don't know if it's love or lust."

Felicia laughs. "Well if you decide to take him back, be careful. Once a man starts hitting on a woman, they don't usually change."

"I know you're right. I need to just leave him alone once and for all."

"Yes, I agree. Girl, there are plenty of fish in the sea. We need to go out for a girl's night. Just us."

"Yes, let's go this weekend."

"Okay, I'll pick you up."

Girls' Night Out

Catherine and Felicia are dressed up in stylish clothing for a girls' night out. They decide to wear the same colors, black and white with silver accessories.

"So where did you say we're going tonight?" Catherine is glad Felicia has a car so they don't have to catch the bus.

"To Club Karaoke on Fifth Avenue."

"Girl, I'm not trying to sing anything."

"Why not? You have a beautiful voice. Let's have some fun."

"Okay."

They arrive at Club Karaoke and walk inside. Heads immediately begin to turn and assess the forms of two beautiful, shapely women. Catherine and Felicia, sharing a knowing glance, smile.

"Let's sit down," Felicia says.

The music is playing soft jazz. The lights are low. Candles are lit on every table, and the ambiance is soothing. As they walk to a table, a waitress comes over to greet them.

"Hello. Welcome to Club Karaoke. May I take your order?"

"Yes, may I have glass of Merlot?" Felicia asks.

"I'll have the same," Catherine says.

"Coming right up."

Felicia notices a man looking at Catherine from a distance across the room.

"Girl, tilt your head slightly to the left. Someone is checking you out."

"Felicia, I don't know if that's a good idea. I think it might be too soon for me to start talking to anyone right now. My heart isn't in it. I just want to have fun tonight," Catherine replies.

"I didn't say you should start a new relationship. But it doesn't hurt to have someone to talk to."

The gentleman to which Felicia is referring approaches their table. He is tall, dark, and handsome, appearing to be in his late thirties.

"Girl, here he comes."

"Hello, ladies. My name is Tony. How are you tonight?"

"We're fine. How are you?" Felicia asks.

"Just wondering what brings two beautiful young ladies like yourselves to my club tonight."

"Your club?"

Tony laughs. "Yes, my club. Can I buy you ladies a drink?" Tony motions for the waitress.

"Whatever they are having, give them another on the house."

"Yes sir."

He addresses Catherine. "Hello, beautiful. This night is almost as beautiful as you are. Care to share a dance with me?"

Catherine looks at Felicia.

"Don't look at me, girl, go ahead. I'll be alright."

By this time, the DJ has changed the record to a different song.

Catherine walks to the dance floor with Tony. They begin to dance to a song by Heatwave. The soft, mellow music plays "Always and Forever."

Tony pulls Catherine closer. They dance slowly and very close.

"What's your name?" Tony asks.

"Catherine."

"A beautiful name for a beautiful woman."

"Thank you. And what's your name?"

"Tony."

"You have a nice name too."

She feels his arms embrace her waist. She smells the scent of his aftershave. He is taller than she is. Catherine rests her head lightly on Tony's shoulder. The strength of his guidance as he leads the dance makes her feel as if she is floating on air. She begins to feel uncomfortable. *Why am I so nervous? Why is he affecting me this way?* Catherine shakes her head. Before the song concludes, she says, "I'm sorry. I can't do this. I'm sorry." She rushes back to her table.

Tony is right behind her. "Catherine, did I do something wrong?"

"No. It's not you. It's just I've recently ended a relationship, and I'm just not ready to go out again."

"No worries, sweetheart, and no pressure. We're just enjoying a dance together on a night where the stars above us dance with us, and although I would love to dance with you all night, I understand your desire to take it slow. May I call you some time?"

"I don't know, Tony."

"Tell you what. Let's just exchange telephone numbers for now, and if ever you want to talk about anything, anything at all, I'll be there to listen."

"Alright, and thank you for understanding."

They exchange telephone numbers, and Tony walks away.

"Girl, what is wrong with you?" Felicia asks.

"I told you I just wanted to have fun, not find myself in the arms of a man," Catherine replies.

"Oh, he must have gotten to you. You were attracted to him. Weren't you?"

"Yes, I'm afraid so."

"What do you mean you're afraid so? Girl, that's good. He might help you get Vic out of your system. Besides, he owns this club too. He has it going on."

Catherine laughs. "I guess he does. But I thought we were coming here to sing."

Felicia laughs. "Okay, let me ask the DJ to add our names to the list."

Chapter Five

Victor's Return

It's been over a month since Catherine last spoke with Victor on the phone. He continues to call, trying to apologize, but she repeatedly hangs up on him. He decides he has exhausted that approach and now it's time to see Catherine face-to-face. Victor pulls up to her house and knocks on the door.

"Who is it?" Michelle asks.

"It's Vic. Hi, Michelle. I need to speak with your mother. It's important." Victor speaks loudly so Michelle can hear him through the closed door.

"Hold on." There is a pause. "Mom, Vic's at the door."

"Okay, I got it. Thanks, Michelle."

Catherine cracks the door open and peeks out.

"What do you want, Vic?"

"You're not answering my calls, so I came over."

"I'm not answering because I don't want to see you. It's over."

"Baby, please. Hear me out. Could you come outside for a minute and sit with me in the car? I don't want the kids to hear our personal business like this."

"Neither do I. You have five minutes. That's it."

Catherine walks outside and gets in the car with Victor.

"Okay, baby. Listen. I know I was bugging that day and I was wrong. Your brothers saw to it that I suffered for it too. I know it was them because Phil was with them. I promise you that it'll never happen again. I've learned my lesson. I swear. I love you, girl. I can't live without you."

Catherine shakes her head. "No you don't. How can you love someone you hurt?"

"I'm an idiot, Catherine. I know it. Believe me. I love you and I don't want to lose you."

Catherine begins to cry. Victor reaches for her and holds her as she cries on his shoulder. He plants kisses on her forehead, her cheeks, and finally her lips. Victor leaves Catherine's home, satisfied he has gotten his woman back. He drives to the drug dealer's house to pick up his next stash.

He hires teenage boys to deliver drugs for him; Darnell is his main runner. After a long day of dealing, he drives back to Catherine's house. It's 11:00 p.m., and the children are in bed. Victor knocks on the door. Catherine is sitting on the couch watching television. She recognizes the knock; she knows it is Victor. She opens the door, and they walk toward the bedroom.

An hour later, Catherine is asleep. Victors goes outside to his car to retrieve his stash. He hides it in the bedroom ceiling tiles.

The Hit and Run

The following morning, Catherine is cooking breakfast while singing in the kitchen.

"Tina, Michelle, Leon? Get up. Breakfast is ready."

Catherine makes a plate for Victor and takes it into the bedroom on a tray.

"Here baby, here you go."

"Thank you. Now that's how you treat your man. Come here. Give me a kiss."

Meanwhile, the children are at the table eating breakfast.

"What are we going to do today?" Michelle asks.

"I don't know about you, but I'm going out with my boyfriend. Maybe you should call your Aunt Stacy. She's closer to your age."

"Okay, I will." Michelle dials Grace's telephone number.

Grace answers. "Hello?"

"Hi, Grandma. Is Stacy there?"

"Hold on, baby. Stacy? Telephone. It's Michelle."

"Hi Michelle."

"Hi Stacy. Let's go to the arcade today. There's one down the street. It has PacMan, Donkey Kong, Centipede, all the best games."

"Okay. You got money? You know those machines aren't free," Stacy says.

"Yeah, I have some change. I'll be right over."

"Okay, see you soon."

Michelle walks down the street heading for the bus stop and sees two girls from her school walking toward her.

"Hi Pat and Rachel. What are y'all doing over this way?"

"What business is it of yours?" Pat asks.

"Oh, I didn't mean anything by it. I was just asking."

"You need to mind your own business."

"Yeah," Rachel says. "We are not your friends. So don't question us about anything, understood?"

"Whatever."

Michelle tries to turn and walk away. All of a sudden, she is shoved into the street, and everything goes black.

The driver of the car that hits Michelle had not seen her. There was no way for him to know what Pat and Rachel were going to do. He pauses momentarily after hitting Michelle but panics and drives off.

Michelle awakens to the sound of sirens. She is lying flat on her back in the street. Neighbors and other drivers have gotten out of their cars and encircle her. There is a crowd of at least fifteen people, all appearing concerned for her.

Michelle slowly opens her eyes. Everything looks blurry. "What happened?"

"Don't move, child," someone says. "The ambulance is here."

The EMS technicians gently lift Michelle and place her on a stretcher. They take her to the nearest hospital.

Michelle has a broken leg, and the opposite knee is bruised and bloody. There is also a large gash on her wrist. A doctor is tending to her injuries. "Hello, young lady. Can you tell me your name?"

Michelle tries to focus, pauses, and replies, "Yes, my name is Michelle."

"Michelle, my name is Dr. Collins. Can you tell me how many fingers I'm holding up?"

"Three."

"Yes, that's correct. Nurse, please step in here. Michelle, do you know who we should contact on your behalf?"

"Yes, please call my mom. Her name is Catherine Hilton, and her number is 555–4321."

"Nurse, did you get that?"

"Yes, I have it, Dr. Collins."

"Please call her mother right away and also be sure to place a call to Child Care Protective Services."

Michelle does not have a clue as to what the agency represents and does not question it. However, somewhere in the back of her mind, she thinks maybe it will protect her from the girls who had done this to her.

The nurse walked down the hall to an office and calls Catherine.

"Ms. Hilton, this is one of the nurses from Memorial Hospital. Your daughter, Michelle, has sustained some serious injuries. Can you come to the hospital right away?"

"For the love of God, what's happened?"

"Ma'am, we're not authorized to discuss this over the telephone. Can you come to the hospital?"

"Yes, I'm on my way." Catherine hangs up. "Vic! Come quick. Michelle is in the hospital. They're telling me she's sustained serious injury. Please drive me there now. Please."

"Alright, calm down. Let me get dressed. I'm coming."

"What's going on, Mom?" Tina asks.

"Your sister's in the hospital. You and your brother stay here. We'll be back."

Catherine and Victor arrive at the hospital and are directed to Michelle's room. When they arrive, Ms. Saunders, the caseworker, meets them at the door.

"Ms. Hilton, I know you're anxious to see your daughter. However, please step into the next room with me. We need to talk first."

"I don't know what's going on here. I have no idea how this could have happened. Please believe me," Catherine says.

"Please calm down, Ms. Hilton. A thorough investigation will be conducted."

The Investigation—Three Weeks Later

Michelle is at home, in bed, with her leg in a cast, and Catherine brings her a glass of orange juice.

"Thanks, Mom."

"You're welcome, baby. Don't worry about a thing. I've filed a police report against the girls who did this to you, and I'm pressing charges."

"Okay, thank you. I don't why they did this to me."

"Neither do I, but we'll get to the bottom of it."

Meanwhile, Ms. Saunders, police officers, and two other caseworkers arrive at Catherine's house. The police knock hard. Catherine wonders who is knocking so hard. "Who is it?"

"It's the police. Open up."

Catherine opens the door, and they almost knock her down, pushing past her. Another officer enters with a police dog. The dog immediately goes to Catherine's bedroom and starts barking at the ceiling. The police find Victor's stash above the ceiling tiles.

"How in the hell did that get there? It's not mine," Catherine exclaims.

"Whose is it?" one of the police officers asks.

"It's Vic's," Leon says.

Victor looks at Leon with intense anger in his eyes.

The police put Victor's hands behind his back and place handcuffs on his wrists. "Sir, you're under arrest."

Victor shakes his head. "What for? I didn't do anything. You can't pin this on me."

Ms. Saunders addresses the other caseworkers. "The two of you need to get the children."

Everything starts to move quickly from this point forward.

Leon yells, "What the hell's going on? I'm not going anywhere."

Tina starts to cry, and Michelle grabs her crutches and slowly limps away, anxious to find a place to hide.

"Everyone, please calm down. We're simply doing our jobs," Ms. Saunders says. "Please cooperate with law enforcement and the caseworkers and everything will go smoothly. Tina, where did Michelle go?"

Tina brushes the tears away.

"I will look for her."

Tina looks for Michelle and finds her crutched against the closet wall, sobbing and attempting to hide behind clothing.

"It's going to be okay, Michelle. Don't cry."

Tina returns with Michelle and caseworkers place the three siblings in separate vehicles and drive in opposite directions.

Addressing Ms. Saunders, Michelle asks, "Where are they taking my sister and brother?"

"Don't worry, Michelle. Everything is going to be fine. You'll see them again."

Youth Group Home

Tina, Leon, and Michelle are sent to different youth group homes awaiting foster care placement. Michelle is eleven, Leon is fifteen, and Tina is sixteen. Since Michelle is the youngest, it is estimated that placement for her will be easier; younger children are placed with foster parents more quickly.

The youth group home where Michelle is taken is for children ages eight to fourteen. Ms. Saunders has made arrangements for Michelle to stay at the youth home through Ms. Dayton, Director of Youth Development. Ms. Saunders drives to the youth group home. She and Michelle get out of the car and walk to the door and ring the bell. A tall, heavyset Caucasian female opens the door.

"May I help you?"

"Yes, you're Ms. Dayton, correct?"

"Yes."

"I'm Ms. Saunders. We spoke on the telephone."

"Oh yes, right this way. Is this Michelle?"

"Yes."

Ms. Dayton escorts them to a room lined with multiple beds with footlockers at the foot of each bed.

"Michelle, you'll be staying with us for a while until suitable placement is found for you."

"No. I want to go home." Michelle cries.

Ms. Saunders tries to console Michelle. "Michelle. It's only temporary, okay? This is a temporary placement."

"Okay, so when can I go home?"

"I'm not sure yet. There are some things that are difficult to explain concerning your home environment. We'll meet again, and counselors will be provided to help you through this transition."

"Transition? What does that mean?"

"Be patient, Michelle. Everything will be explained. For now, go rest. I'll have someone call your doctor to make sure you have medication for your injuries. For now, please go lie down. We'll talk again soon."

Ms. Saunders leaves the building as Ms. Dayton escorts Michelle to her bed.

"Michelle, we'll go shopping for clothing tomorrow."

"I have clothes at home. I want to go home."

"I'll leave you for now. In the morning, I'll introduce you to your fellow roommates," Ms. Dayton replies.

The Following Day

At 8:00 a.m., Ms. Dayton awakens the children and instructs them to shower and change. Since it is summer break, children are allowed to sleep until 8:00. Breakfast is served at 9:00.

After breakfast, the children are told to report to the conference room for Michelle's introduction.

"Everyone, this is Michelle. She's going to be staying with us for a while. Please say hello to Michelle."

"Hello," everyone says.

After introductions, Ms. Dayton gave Michelle a tour of the building. Outside their bedroom, children were allowed to go into the cafeteria, the conference room, the library, and the game room. The game room was the most popular room since it had a ping-pong table, a television, and three video arcade machines.

Michelle went to the game room. Cedric, a thirteen-year-old boy, taps Michelle on the shoulder. Michelle turns.

"Hi," Cedric says.

"Hi."

"Are you scared?"

"No."

"It's okay to be scared if you are. Everybody is at first."

"I'm not scared. I just want to go home."

"We all want to go home. But for now, we have to make the best of it. So if you need a friend, I'm here. You can talk to me."

"Thanks, Cedric. You're very nice. I appreciate that."

"Do you know how to play ping-pong?"

"Not really."

"Let me teach you," Cedric says.

"Not today. Maybe tomorrow."

"Okay, tomorrow it is."

The remainder of the day consisted of workshops associated with mentoring, positive behavior support and group therapy. Group therapy was facilitated by Ms. Dayton.

"Alright, everyone, it is time for us to get to know each other a little better. We are going to have group discussion where everyone begins by introducing themselves. After you introduce yourself, please share a few details about personal likes and dislikes. Also, we will discuss motivators as well as 'pet peeves,' i.e., triggers to avoid."

Each child took a turn sharing personal information about themselves; however when it was Michelle's turn to speak, she remained silent.

Ms. Dayton says, "Give her time, everyone. She will come around."

Michelle's New Friend

On the following day, the children are called for breakfast. Cedric joins Michelle in the cafeteria for breakfast.

"Good morning, Michelle."

"Good morning, Cedric."

"How do you feel today?" Cedric asks.

"I guess better than yesterday."

"Good. After breakfast, join me in the game room. You do remember, you promised me a game of ping-pong?"

"Yes, I did. Didn't I?"

"Yep."

"Okay, you're on," Michelle replies.

Cedric told jokes as he played ping-pong with Michelle. Although she was reluctant to open up to anyone, eventually Cedric's jokes tickled her and she laughed.

The Courthouse

The telephone rings in Catherine's home. Catherine is crying and does not answer it. Her children are gone, and Victor is in jail. She doesn't want to talk to anyone. The telephone continues to ring. Finally, she picks up the handset.

"Hello?"

"Hello, may I speak with Ms. Hilton? This is Ms. Saunders, caseworker from Child Care Protective Services."

"Yes, Ms. Saunders, this is Ms. Hilton. What else do you want from me? You've taken my children. You've taken everything. What else do you want?"

"Ms. Hilton, it's not my goal to take anything from anyone. I'm only doing what's in the best interest of the children. I need you to understand that. I'm calling because a custody hearing has been scheduled one week from today at 8:00 a.m. at the courthouse. If you don't have an attorney, one will be provided to you. A letter with details was mailed out a few days ago. You should be receiving it any day now."

"I'll check my mailbox, and I'll see you next week. Good-bye." Catherine hangs up.

One Week Later

Catherine is in the courtroom. The referee announces the presence of the judge.

"All rise. The Honorable Judge Balton, presiding."

Judge Balton taps his gavel and takes his seat.

"You may be seated."

"In the matter of the State vs. Catherine Hilton on the counts of child neglect and endangerment, how do you plead?"

"Not guilty," Catherine says.

"Counsel, you may present your arguments."

The prosecuting attorney, representing the state, provides damaging evidence to support allegations of child neglect and endangerment.

The court-appointed defense attorney does little to support Catherine's not-guilty plea. Judge Balton issues his final ruling.

"In the matter of the State vs. Catherine Hilton on the counts of child neglect and endangerment, the court finds the defendant guilty on all charges. The children will be remanded to the custody of the state and are hereby deemed wards of the state. This hearing is adjourned."

Catherine leaves the courthouse in tears. When she arrives home, she calls Felicia.

"They took my babies, Felicia. They took my babies."

"Catherine, don't cry. I'll be right over."

When Felicia arrives at Catherine's house, Catherine opens the door. Her eyes are red and swollen from crying. Felicia grabs her friend and hugs her.

"Listen, Catherine. This is what I need you to do. Remember Tony, the guy from Club Karaoke?"

"Yes."

"Call him. Tell him what's happened. I'm sure he'll be willing to help you."

"No, Felicia. I can't do that. I don't even know him."

"So what? It's time get to know him. Call him now."

Catherine dials Tony's number. After two rings, he answers.

"Hello?"

"Hello, Tony?"

"Yes, this is he. May I ask who is calling?"

"You probably don't remember me. I'm Catherine from Club Karaoke."

"Yes, I remember. I could never forget such a beautiful face."

"Thank you for saying that. With everything I'm facing right now, I really don't feel beautiful at all. I'm hoping you might be able to help me."

"Well, in that case, how about having dinner with me? You can tell me all about it."

"Alright. Can you pick me up?"

"Sure. What's your address?"

Catherine gives Tony her address.

"Alright, I'll see you at eight, Catherine."

"Alright." Catherine returns the handset to its receiver.

"Now was that so hard?" Felicia asks.

"No." Catherine laughs. Her laughter has the sound of grief in it. She sighs.

"Have you heard anything more about Vic?"

"I heard he might get five to ten years."

"Maybe that's a good thing, Catherine. He was taking you down. It's time for you to move on with your life and settle down with a good man. I think Tony might be that man."

"I hope you're right. I guess I need to find something to wear tonight. Felicia, thank you. You're such a good friend to me. Thank you so much."

"You're welcome. Now let me get out of here while you prepare for your date. Love you, girl. Have fun."

The Date

Tony arrives at Catherine's house promptly at 8:00. Catherine is nervous. She has never had a man come to her home after only just having met him. But she has a good feeling about him and knows he is a businessman who is very polite and courteous.

Tony knocks on the door. Catherine asks, "Who is it?"

"It's Tony."

Catherine opens the door. She is dressed in an all-black evening gown with silver-studded black shoes, silver handbag, and silver accessories.

"Wow," Tony exclaims. "You are beautiful."

"Thank you."

"Shall we go? Your chariot awaits."

Tony opens the passenger door of his BMW for Catherine. As she gets into the car, she thinks, *I knew he was a gentleman. Maybe, just maybe, my luck is about to change.*

Tony pulls up to the Flaming Embers, a fine-food restaurant in the heart of the city. He opens the door for Catherine and escorts her inside.

"Party for two?" the waiter asks. "Right this way, sir."

The waiter escorts Tony and Catherine to their table. Tony pulls out her chair, and she sits. Tony begins to look at the wine list.

The waiter returns.

"Please bring a glass of your best house wine for the lady."

"Red or white?" the waiter asks.

"Good question. Which do you prefer, Catherine?"

"Red, please."

"Yes ma'am. Let me get that for you."

They looked at the menus. Catherine orders a T-bone steak with baked potato and salad, and Tony orders Lobster in creamy butter sauce with Crab legs and pasta.

"Alright, now that we have taken care of the little things, tell me what's on your mind."

Catherine spends the next fifteen minutes trying to summarize the unfortunate events that led to her losing her children.

"I'm sorry. I don't mean to burden you with all my troubles. I'm sure this is too much for anyone to handle, especially on a first date."

"Not at all, Catherine. It sounds like you need help; a true damsel in distress. I don't run from challenges. I face them head-on."

"You're so kind. I'm trying so hard not to cry right now. It's all been so overwhelming."

"I understand. However, I have one question for you, and I really need an honest answer. If Victor gets out of jail in the next five years, are you planning to take him back again?"

"No, it's really over this time. He's caused me to lose my children. I'll never take him back again, never."

"That's all I needed to know. I'll help you get your children back."

"Really? How?"

"I have connections. Leave that to me. I'll keep you posted as developments unfold."

"Tony, there's something important you should know. I don't want there to be any secrets or surprises."

"Yes, Catherine, what is it? You can tell me anything."

"Sometimes, Vic and I would take certain narcotics together. This is probably why he felt so comfortable bringing it to my home. However, I never gave him permission to stash drugs in my house, in my bedroom. I promise I didn't know it was there."

"Thank you for being honest with me, Catherine."

"There's one more thing. After I tell you this, I'll understand if it's too much to deal with. But I feel I must tell you everything in order to regain full custody of my children without any hiccups."

"Go on."

"I think I may have a problem with drugs. I've come to this conclusion because whenever I become depressed or discouraged, I find myself turning to that as an easy fix. I know the problem will still be there when it's all said and done, but sometimes I feel the need to escape. Also, although I was not charged with drug possession, I know I'm partially responsible because of my lifestyle."

"Catherine, would you be willing to admit yourself into a drug rehabilitation center?"

"If that means getting my children back, yes I would."

"Then let's start there, and I'll get the ball rolling."

"One last question. If I'm in rehab, how will I be able to make court appearances?"

"Don't worry about that. An attorney can arrange for temporary discharges for court appearances."

"Alright. Thank you so much. I don't know how I'll ever repay you."

"It's not necessary. Now let's enjoy the rest of our evening."

"Thank you, Tony."

Chapter Six

Foster Home Number One

Within a few short months, each child is placed in a different foster home. Michelle is placed in the foster care of Kevin and Emma Johnson.

"Hello, Michelle, it's so nice to meet you. We finally have a playmate for our only child, Jessica. You and Jessica are going to be great friends. I just know it. Welcome to our home," Mrs. Johnson says.

"Thank you."

"Jessica, please show Michelle to her room and help her unpack her things. After you've finished, meet me in the study where we can go over house rules."

"Okay," Jessica says.

Twenty minutes later, Jessica and Michelle join Mr. and Mrs. Johnson in the study.

"Alright, Michelle, we have house rules. I'd like you to read them and sign and date the document."

Michelle reads the document. There were over twenty different rules. There were so many that Michelle becomes uncomfortable.

"Are you finished?"

"Yes."

"Okay, sign it and give it to me, please."

Michelle signs the document and returns it to Mrs. Johnson.

Later, that evening after dinner, Mrs. Johnson says, "Alright, girls, it's almost eight. I need you to clean the kitchen, iron your clothes for church tomorrow, and turn down your bedding. Bedtime is nine, and there's absolutely no talking after nine, understood?"

"Yes," replies Jessica.

"Yes ma'am," replies Michelle.

The girls do as they were told, and approximately thirty minutes later, Jessica says, "It's only 8:30, Michelle. We still have thirty minutes left. Let's watch television in our room."

For the next thirty minutes, the girls watch television. At 9:00 sharp, Mrs. Johnson is at their bedroom door.

"Lights out, girls. Be sure to go to the restroom before you go to bed. Remember, no talking."

Jessica and Michelle have bunk beds in one bedroom. "I sleep on the top," Jessica says. "You have to take the bottom bunk."

"No problem," Michelle says.

At 9:10, Jessica whispers, "Michelle, tomorrow, I'm going to show you my doll collection. I have dolls in every color and with great outfits from all over the world, China, Europe, you name it."

"Really, oh wow. That sounds like fun. I can't wait until tomorrow."

At that moment, Mrs. Johnson returns with a belt in her hand.

"Michelle, I know you're new here, but you have to learn the rules early. I said no talking after nine." Mrs. Johnson begins to hit Michelle with the belt.

"Stop it! Stop it!" Michelle screams.

"Momma, please don't hit her. She just got here," Jessica yells.

"Hush your mouth, Jessica. She has to learn early. Spare the rod, spoil the child."

Michelle softly cries herself to sleep.

The next day, the Johnsons, Michelle, and Jessica prepare for church. When they arrive, Mrs. Johnson escorts them to a pew, and Mr. Johnson hands them a book of hymns.

"Girls, listen closely to the speakers. They will instruct you on what page to turn to for our hymns today."

"Yes sir," both girls reply.

The Connection

Tony is in his office at Club Karaoke. He dials the number for Bill Michaels, an attorney.

"Hello, Attorney Michaels here."

"Hi, Bill. It's Tony. How are you?"

"I'm fine, Tony. What's up?"

"I need a favor."

"What can I do for you?"

"I have a friend who recently lost her children to foster care. I need you to look into the case and see if there are any circumstances surrounding the case that you could use for appeal."

"Alright. I'll need all the details. Leave nothing out. I'll also need to meet with this friend."

"I'll set up a meeting. Thanks, Bill."

"No problem, Tony. I got you."

Tony calls Catherine.

"Hello?"

"Hi, Catherine. How are you?"

"As well as can be expected, Tony. How are you?"

"I'm good. I've got great news for you."

"Really?"

"I have a friend who's an attorney. His name is Bill Michaels, and he'd like to meet with you to discuss the details surrounding your child custody case. When are you available?"

"Well, I've called the rehab center, and I was planning to admit myself Monday morning, but I could wait until after our meeting with Attorney Michaels."

"Alright. I'll check with Bill to see when there's an opening on his calendar and get back to you."

"Thank you, Tony."

"No problem, Catherine. I'll be in touch."

The Next Day

Tony dials Attorney Michaels's number.

"Hello?"

"Hello, Bill. Tony here."

"How are you, Tony?"

"I'm good. Listen, I spoke to my friend, Catherine Hilton. She's available to meet with you whenever you have an opening."

"Okay. Hold on. Let me take a look. Alright, tell her to meet me at my office on Wednesday of next week. I have an opening at 1:00 p.m."

"Sounds good. We'll be there."

"We? I take it you have a personal interest in this friend."

"I do."

"Well, that's different. Why didn't you say so?" Bill laughs. "I'll do my best to help her."

"Thanks, Bill. See you Wednesday."

The Following Wednesday

Catherine and Tony arrive at Bill Michaels's office and are escorted in by the receptionist.

"Good morning, Tony." Bill pauses to acknowledge Catherine. "I take it you're the lovely Catherine, yes?"

Catherine smiles. "Thank you for the compliment. Hello, Mr. Michaels."

"Thank you for meeting with us today," Tony says.

"You're welcome. Please have a seat, both of you. Alright, let's get down to business. I have reviewed your case files, and I see that issues surrounding the charges are not direct neglect or endangerment but circumstances that appear as accidents. I also see that you were not charged for the drugs found in your home. However, a man by the name of Victor Sinclair is serving time for the drug charge today, correct?"

"Yes."

"May I ask who Victor is to you?"

"He was my boyfriend."

"Okay, I see. Now in the event I'm able to help you regain custody of your children, do you plan to continue a relationship with Victor when he gets out of jail? Before you answer, I'm asking only because it appears he may pose a problem if it's found he's returned to the home. We don't want to go through this process only to lose your children again."

"I understand. I assure you I have no intention of allowing Victor back into my home ever again."

"Alright, I'll proceed with the appeal and will call you when the court date is scheduled."

"Thank you," Catherine says.

"Alright, Tony? Catherine? Are we all set?"

"Yes, thanks, Bill. We'll talk again soon. Take care for now."

Catherine and Tony leave the office. Catherine turns to Tony and embraces him tightly. "Thank you so much, Tony. Thank you."

Tony draws her close to himself. Their eyes lock for a moment and then she steps away from him. He reaches for her hand and Catherine extends hers.

"Everything is going to be alright, Catherine." They return to the vehicle and he takes her home.

The following week, she admits herself into a rehabilitation center.

The Foster Sisters

Michelle and Jessica are playing jump rope outside.

"Michelle, I bet I can jump longer than you can."

"No, you can't," Michelle says.

"Watch! One, two, three—" Jessica counts her jumps up to twenty-five before she trips the rope.

"Okay, my turn."

Michelle counts her jumps up to nineteen before she trips the rope.

"Told ya," Jessica says.

"Aww, you're lucky. I'll beat you next time."

Jessica laughs. "Let's go play with my doll collection."

Michelle and Jessica play with the doll collection for nearly twenty-five minutes. They change the dolls' outfits and have a tea party. There are cups and dresses and toys strewn all over the bedroom. They are having so much fun. Mrs. Johnson arrives at the bedroom door.

"Look at this mess. Clean this up immediately. Who did this? I know Jessica didn't. She knows better than to make this kind of a mess."

Mrs. Johnson grabs Michelle by the shoulder, pulling her dress. "Little girl, you had better learn how to conduct yourself in my home or your behind is going to be black and blue."

"What did I do now?" Michelle asks.

Mrs. Johnson slaps her face. "Don't talk back to me."

"I want to go home." Michelle cries. "I want to go home."

"You are home. There is no one else out there who will take you, so get over it."

Mrs. Johnson leaves the bedroom.

"I'll help you clean up, Michelle. It's going to be okay."

"Thanks, Jessica."

The Appeal—Three Months Later

Catherine is discharged from the rehabilitation center and is returning home. She feels like a new woman, clean and drug-free for three months. Now it is time to remove all temptation from her life. Catherine arrives at her home, opens the door, and walks to the bathroom medicine cabinet. She feels lucky that the items in there were not confiscated when the police were there. She knows it's time to get rid of them once and for all. Catherine grabs the items, throws them in a trash bag, and takes the bag outside to the dumpster.

One Week Later

The telephone rings. Catherine picks up.

"Hello, Catherine."

"Hello, Tony. It's so nice to hear your voice."

"Yours too, lady. I called the rehab center. When I asked to speak with you, I was told you were discharged."

"Yes, I was discharged last week."

"Why didn't you call me?"

"I'm getting my life in order, Tony, and I had to remove all the things that took it from me."

"Good. I'm glad to hear that. Listen, we have a court date."

"We do?"

"Yes, Friday of next week at eight a.m. Can you make it?"

"Of course I can. I wouldn't miss it for the world."

"Good. I'll pick you up Friday."

"Thank you. See you Friday."

Friday Morning

Catherine and Tony arrive at the courthouse. Attorney Michaels is there waiting for them. He waves them over to a bench outside the courtroom. "Good morning. Let's talk for a moment before we go in."

"Good morning," Catherine says.

Tony and Bill shake hands.

"I want you to know how I'd like to proceed with the appeal. Catherine, I don't want you to testify. Are you okay with that?"

"Yes."

"I'll present your case and the circumstantial evidence previously submitted. I found that it doesn't prove guilt without reasonable doubt."

"Thank you."

"Alright, let's go inside."

Catherine, Tony, and Bill go to the front of the courtroom and take seats. Fifteen minutes later, Judge Balton arrives.

"All rise. The Honorable Judge Balton, presiding."

Judge Balton taps his gavel. "You may be seated. In the matter of the State vs. Catherine Hilton on the counts of child neglect and endangerment, I would like the attorneys to approach the bench."

The prosecuting attorney and Attorney Michaels approach the bench to present arguments to support their cases. The prosecuting attorney presents the same argument presented in the first hearing. However, Attorney Michaels objects to this argument by placing emphasis on incidents that had direct bearing on Michelle's accidents. He further points out that Catherine was not arrested for anything and had no prior history of child endangerment or neglect.

After hearing both attorneys' arguments, Judge Balton replies, "We will recess for one hour, and I will return with my decision."

One Hour Later

"In the matter of the State vs. Catherine Hilton on the counts of child neglect and endangerment, the court finds the defendant not guilty."

"Yes!" Catherine exclaims. "Thank you. Oh my God, thank you."

Tony and Bill shake hands.

"Attorney Michaels will call Ms. Saunders, Catherine. He will make arrangements to get your kids back. Thanks, Bill." Tony says.

They leave the courthouse.

Chapter Seven

Custody Regained

Attorney Michaels places a telephone call to Ms. Saunders. He conveys the outcome of the hearing. He also informs her that a copy of the final judgment of appeal will be forwarded to her. Upon receipt, Ms. Saunders calls Catherine to arrange for return of the children. A few weeks later, Ms. Saunders pulls up at Catherine's house. Michelle, Tina, and Leon are in her car. She knocks on the door.

"Who is it?" Catherine asks.

"Ms. Saunders."

Catherine flings the door open.

"My babies!" She hugs and kisses her children, and they all cry together.

"I missed you so much, Momma," Michelle says.

"Yes, I thought we'd never come home again," Tina says.

Leon shakes head. "Wow, I can't believe we're home."

"My babies are home."

The Romance

Catherine's telephone rings. "Hello?"

"Hello, sweetheart. It's Tony."

"Hi Tony! How are you?

"I'm fine and you?"

"Tony, I'm so indebted to you. You have no idea how much I appreciate you. You gave me my children back. Thank you." Catherine's voice is shaky with emotion and full with tears of joy.

"Don't cry, baby. It's over now. Now maybe you and I can take our relationship to the next level. Are you ready for that?"

"Yes, Tony, I'm ready."

"I know it's too soon for you to go away with me for a week or two, as it is really important for you to reconnect with your children right now. Therefore, I have another idea."

"Yes?"

"I have a little place off the lake. It's my vacation house during the holidays. Let me take you there this weekend just for one night. Let me hold you in my arms and love you."

"Yes." Catherine's voice is breathy. "Yes."

"I'll come for you around ten Friday night. We'll slip away together, and I'll have you home by morning."

Friday Night

It's 9:55 p.m., and Catherine peers out the window looking for Tony's BMW. Tony arrives at 10:00 p.m. sharp. Catherine leaves a note for the children on the refrigerator in case they awake. She exits the house and locks the door.

Tony steps out of the car and opens the passenger door for her. She slips in beside him, and they drive for more than forty miles until they come to the lake house, which sits high off the rocks. As she steps out of the car, she can see the water splash against the rocks.

"It's beautiful, Tony."

"You're beautiful, Catherine."

Tony reaches for Catherine's hand. She extends it, and he closes his over hers. As they walk toward the house, Catherine observes the view of the winding staircase and the crystal chandelier visible from the massive window facing the lake. They ascend the staircase. Tony opens the door for her. Catherine walks inside. Tony walks to the wine rack and selects a fine bottle of vintage red wine. He pops the cork. He walks to the bar and grabs two glasses and half-fills each glass. Passing Catherine a glass, he says, "Here you are, sweetheart. You do like red?"

"Yes I do. Thank you."

Tony walks toward the stereo and puts on an album by Bill Withers. They sit close to one another as they sip wine, talk, and listen to Bill Withers sing, "Ain't No Sunshine When She's Gone."

Catherine observes a cascading water fountain adjacent to the fireplace and watches the water glisten off the pebbles.

She sighs. "This is so beautiful Tony. You have a lovely place."

"Are you hungry? I haven't been here for a few months, but I can certainly have something delivered," Tony says.

"Yes, please. That would be nice."

"What do you have a taste for?"

"I'm not sure. It really doesn't matter. Whatever you want is fine, Tony."

"I want you, Catherine."

Catherine lowers her eyes.

Tony reaches for her chin and lifts it up gently.

"Do you want me, Catherine?"

"Yes I do, Tony, very much."

Tony stands and reaches for her hand. Catherine takes it, and he leads her to the bedroom. Catherine's gown has more than twenty buttons down the back. He unbuttons each button very slowly. Underneath Catherine's gown, she has on black lace undergarments. He continues to undress her until she stands before him naked.

"You're a beautiful woman, Catherine." Tony begins to kiss her from the top of her head to her neck, her breasts, and lower. Catherine moans. He picks her up and gently places her on the bed. Undressing himself, he joins her on the bed. He continues to kiss and caress her.

"Tony, please. I don't how much more I can take."

"Hush, my love." Tony enters her slowly, moving in motion with her hips. She moistens beneath him. He cups her breast and teases it with his tongue. She moans. Then in one long thrust, he buries himself in her. Each thrust seems to plunge deeper and deeper. As their passion builds, their breathing becomes labored. Catherine screams as she explodes in pure ecstasy.

One Hour Later

"I'm starving," Catherine says.

"I guess we never got to eat dinner. What time is it?"

"Almost midnight."

"My club is still open. I'll have Chauncey, my assistant, deliver us something."

"Baby, he'll have to drive forty miles."

"Don't worry. Chauncey is my right-hand man. Believe me, he's driven farther." Tony laughs.

"Okay." Catherine laughs also. "Tony, you're the most romantic man I've ever known, generous and kind-hearted too. How did I get so lucky?"

"I'm the lucky one, Catherine." Tony pauses and moves a strand of hair from her face. He kisses her once more and calls Chauncey.

Chauncey is in the office at Club Karaoke, putting cash in the safe. The telephone rings. "Hello, Club Karaoke. May I help you?"

"Hi Chauncey. It's Tony."

"Tony, where are you, man?"

"Catherine and I are at the lake house. There's nothing here to eat. Could you bring us something from the club? Most places are closed now."

"Sure. What do you want?"

"It doesn't matter. Just make sure it's fresh and hot."

"You got it," Chauncey says.

Forty minutes later, Chauncey arrives with the food and rings the doorbell. Catherine runs back to the bedroom.

"Why are you rushing off, love?" Tony asks.

"I'm not dressed appropriately, and I don't want Chauncey to see me. I'll be in the bedroom."

Tony laughs as Catherine closes the bedroom door.

Tony opens the door for Chauncey.

"Hi, Chauncey. Thanks for coming. I know it's late, so here's a little something for the inconvenience."

Tony hands Chauncey some cash. Chauncey slips it into his pocket.

"No problem, man. You're welcome. Y'all have a nice night."

"We shall," Tony says. "Thanks again, Chauncey."

Tony takes the food into the bedroom and speaks to Catherine. "Since it's getting so late, I know we'll oversleep if I don't set this alarm clock, and I know you need to get home before the children awake," Tony says.

"Yes I do."

"I'll set the alarm for six. We don't have long to sleep," Tony says.

"I know, and as much as I don't like to eat before bedtime, it just can't be helped tonight."

"So true."

Returning Home

The alarm clock rings at 6:00 a.m. Tony and Catherine awake. Catherine stretches her arms to the sky and yawns while Tony shuts off the clock.

"Good morning, sweetheart. How are you this fine morning?"

"Sleepy," Catherine says.

"Yes I know. Let's take a shower together and get dressed."

"Together?" Catherine asks.

"Yes, why not?"

"I'm afraid you're going to start something we don't have time to finish." Catherine laughs.

"You're probably right. I need to get you home."

"Yes, so I'll shower quickly and be right out," Catherine says.

"Where's the fun in that?" Tony laughs.

Forty-five minutes later, Tony and Catherine are ready to leave the lake house. They drive back to Catherine's place and arrive at approximately 7:30 a.m. Catherine gets out of the car and walks up the staircase to her home. Tony follows her to the door. She gently places the key in the cylinder and opens the door. She turns and looks at Tony before entering. "Good night, Tony. Thank you for a beautiful night."

"Thank you, Catherine. The pleasure was all mine. I love you, lady."

"I love you too, Tony."

Tony reaches for her waist and pulls her close to him for a kiss. "Good night, my love."

"Good night, Tony."

Catherine steps inside and closes the door gently behind her. She tiptoes to Michelle's room, peeks inside, and sees she is fast asleep. She peeks inside Tina's room. Tina is not there. Last, she peeks inside Leon's room and sees him playing video games. He turns as soon as the light from the hallway enters his room.

"Where have you been, young lady? I've been worried sick," Leon says.

"Hi, Leon. I left a note on the refrigerator. Didn't you see it?"

"Yes, but it didn't say where you were going. You can't be leaving us, Mom. We just got you back."

"I'm not leaving, Leon. I met someone, and his name is Tony. Tony is the main reason I was able to get you all back. Without him, none of this would have been possible."

"I need to meet this Tony. I want to thank him personally."

"You will. I promise. Now where's Tina?"

"Oh, she called her boyfriend as soon as she got home. I think he came and picked her up."

"Oh really? Here we go. I'll talk to her as soon she gets here. She's been gone all night?"

"Yeah. I woke up myself around three and went to the kitchen to get some water and saw your note. Haven't been able to sleep since."

"Okay. Get your some sleep now, and thank you for keeping an eye on your little sister."

"You're welcome, Mom."

Catherine walks into her bedroom and lies on the bed. She reflects on her night with Tony. Just then, she hears the front door. Tina is home.

"Tina, where have you been?" Catherine asks.

"I went out with a friend."

"At this hour? Have you been gone all night?"

"I didn't even know how late it was, and then I fell asleep on the couch."

"Okay, okay. You're home now, but please, starting from this day forward, no more sneaking out of the house, no more fighting, okay? If you promise to change your behavior, I promise to work on mine as well, deal?"

"Deal," Tina says.

Chapter Eight

The Proposal

One year later, Michelle, Tina, and Leon have accepted Tony as the new man in their mother's life. Things are going well for the family, and everyone is working toward building healthier relationships.

Catherine's telephone rings. "Hello?"

"Hello, sweetheart. I've planned a special dinner for us tonight. Can I pick you up around eight?"

"Yes. Where are we going?"

"All in due time. I'll see you at eight."

Catherine laughs. "Okay, now I'm curious, but alright. See you at eight."

She hangs up the telephone.

"Tina, Michelle, Leon, come here, please."

The children meet their mom in the living room. They are puzzled.

"What's up, Mom?" Leon asks.

"Tony has planned a special dinner for me tonight. I'm not sure where we're going yet, but I know wherever it is, it'll be nice. You know, he's such a great guy, and I think we're all lucky to have him in our lives."

"I wouldn't say all that," Tina says jokingly.

"He's really nice, Tina. I like him," Michelle says.

"He's alright," Leon says.

"Thank you, guys. Tina, can you fix dinner tonight for the three of you? I have to start getting ready."

"Okay, no problem, Mom."

"And, Tina remember our deal. Please do not leave."

"I won't. I promise."

"Thank you."

Catherine reflects on her wardrobe and realizes she does not have much to choose from. From what Tony said, it sounded formal. However, Catherine has only one formal black evening gown. She really does not want to wear that again but does not know what else to select that will be befitting the occasion. She chooses the black evening gown again.

Two Hours Later

Tony pulls up to Catherine's house and rings the doorbell. Catherine reluctantly opens the door, knowing Tony would recognize the gown from the last time she wore it. "Hi, Tony. Listen, before you say anything, I don't have many options to choose from in the wardrobe department, especially in formal wear. This is about it."

"Not a problem, Catherine. You're beautiful no matter what you have on or don't have on." Tony laughs. "But if it makes you uncomfortable, let's do something about that right now. Let's go shopping."

"No. You don't have to do that, Tony."

"It's no problem at all. It's just a small change of plans."

Tony drives to Saks Fifth Avenue. When they arrive, Catherine gasps.

"Are you kidding me? Do you have any idea how much things cost in there?"

"As a matter of fact I do." Tony laughs. "Come with me, Catherine."

Thoughts were running through Tony's mind. *Saks Fifth Avenue is the perfect place to propose. I had initially planned for dinner, but this is even better.*

"Alright, Catherine, I want you to find something attractive. Don't look at the cost. Just look for design, feel the material, try it on, and see how it feels on your skin, alright?"

"Alright."

"Now I have only one request."

"Yes?"

"I want you to come out of the dressing room and model it for me."

"Okay." Catherine smiles. "This may take a while."

"No problem. I'll wait here until you return."

"Okay. I'll try not to take too long."

Catherine looks around the store for more than twenty minutes until the most stunning gown she has ever seen catches her eye. The gown is cream colored; the trim of the neckline, cuffs and bodice is black. The back of the gown dips down to the waist to expose a bare back. Catherine thinks, *Okay, I promised I wouldn't look at the price.*

Catherine drapes the gown across her arm and proceeds to the shoe department. After the salesperson helps her find the perfect shoes to match the gown, Catherine heads for the dressing room.

When she steps out, Tony sees her and walks toward her.

"Stunning, absolutely stunning. Please don't move, Catherine."

"Why?"

Tony kneels on one knee and pulls a small black box from his suit coat pocket. He opens the box and presents it to Catherine. "Catherine, my love, will you marry me?"

Heads begin to turn as passersby observe the proposal. People begin to stare. Ooohs and ahhhs are heard in the background.

"Yes, Tony, I will marry you."

There is applause. Tony stands and pulls Catherine close to him, and they kiss.

Tina's Boyfriend

Catherine's telephone rings.

"Michelle, can you get that? I'm doing something right now," Tina says.

"No, because it's not for me. It's always for you, Momma, or Leon."

"Michelle, please and hurry up before it stops ringing."

"Okay." Michelle answers the telephone. "Hello? Who is this?"

"It's Gary. Is Tina home?"

"Hold on. Tina? Gary's on the phone."

Tina rushes to the telephone.

"Hi, Gary."

"Hi Tina. What ya doing?"

"Nothing really. Just thinking about you."

"Let's go out tonight."

"I want to go, but I promised my mom I wouldn't sneak out anymore. Why don't you come over for dinner and I can finally introduce you?"

"You want me to meet your mother?"

"Why not?"

"Alright, I guess so. What time?"

"Tomorrow at six."

"Alright, see you then."

Tony pulls up to Catherine house and drops her off. Catherine is smiling from ear to ear as she walks into her house. She wants to share her good news with the children. "Tina, Michelle, Leon? Everyone, please come here for a moment."

"What is it, Mom?" Leon asks.

"I'm getting married. Tony proposed, and I'm getting married."

"Congratulations, Mom. I'm so happy for you," Tina says. "I have good news too."

"Yes? What's your good news?"

"Gary is coming for dinner tomorrow at six."

"Really? Well I guess it's about time I met with this young man. What are you cooking?" Catherine laughs.

"Me? I thought you were going to cook so it could be special."

"He's your boyfriend, not mine." Catherine laughs again.

The Next Day, 6:25 p.m.

There is a knock at Catherine's door.

"Who is it?" Tina asks.

"It's Gary."

Tina opens the door. "You're late."

"Sorry. At least I came. Meeting someone's mom for the first time isn't easy, you know."

"Alright, that may be true. So you get a pass this time." Tina laughs.

"Thank you," Gary says.

"Mom?" Tina yells.

"Yes, Tina. What is it?"

"Please come here."

Catherine enters the living room.

Tina says, "This is Gary. Gary, this is my mother. Her name is Catherine Hilton."

Gary extends his hand. "Hello, Ms. Hilton. Nice to meet you."

Catherine shakes his hand. "Nice to finally meet you as well, Gary. Welcome to my home." "Okay, Gary, please take a seat in the living room while I prepare the table," Tina says.

Gary sits down on the living room sofa. Leon comes out of his room and walks toward him.

"What's up, man? How've you been?"

"Alright, I guess. Just met your mom."

"I heard. Funny, I've seen your raggedy behind a million times." Leon laughs. "Now you're trying to come over here and act all proper."

"Nah, nah. I'm just trying to be respectful."

"Oh now you want to be respectful. Okay, better late than never."

Gary laughs. "Right."

Tina comes out of the kitchen. "Okay everyone, dinner is ready. Please wash your hands."

Everyone takes turns washing hands in the bathroom before sitting at the table. Tina has prepared meatloaf, mashed potatoes with gravy, and string beans, which are all on the table.

"You cooked this?" Gary asks.

"Yes sir."

"It smells good." Gary takes a bite. "It is good."

"Thank you," Tina says.

"Gary, thank you for joining us for dinner," Catherine says. "May I ask a question?"

"Mom, please don't drill him," Tina says.

"I'm not. Relax, Tina. It's just a question."

"Yes ma'am, you can ask a question."

"Thank you. Now you know Tina is only sixteen. How old are you?"

"I'm seventeen, Ms. Hilton."

"Alright, well please remember you both have your whole lives ahead of you so there's no need to rush into anything, correct?"

"Yes ma'am."

"Mom, please," Tina pleads.

"I'm done, Tina. Calm down." Catherine laughs as everyone enjoys the meal.

The Customer

Tony is in his office reviewing the books. He hears some kind of disturbance coming from the bar area. He picks up the telephone and calls Chauncey. "What's going on?" Tony asks.

"Tony, you need to get out here. A customer has had too much to drink, and the bartender cut him off. Now he's ranting and raving like some kind of lunatic."

"Where's security?"

"I called him on the radio. He's not answering."

"I'll be right there."

Tony approaches the bar. "Sir, I understand you have a problem with the bartender and would like another drink."

"That's right. I don't know what the damn problem is." The customer slurs his words.

"Sir, according to state law, we have the right to cut off drinks if we feel a customer has become overly impaired. In fact, let me call you a cab because we can't allow you to leave in your condition."

"You can't what? Man, you better move the hell out of my way."

Tony attempts to restrain the man just as security is walking toward them. One shot is fired. Tony slumps to the floor.

"Oh my God! Someone call nine-one-one now!"

The bartender makes the call, and an ambulance arrives within ten minutes. EMS staff immediately place Tony on the stretcher and put him in the back of the ambulance.

"I have to ride with you guys. I have to know he's okay," Chauncey says.

"Alright, get in."

The driver turns on his siren and speeds to the nearest hospital. While in route, EMS staff attempt to control the bleeding from Tony's wound. An oxygen mask is placed over his face. Ten minutes later, the ambulance arrives at the hospital. It is too late. Tony is gone.

Catherine's telephone rings.

"Hello, Catherine speaking."

"Hi, Catherine. This is Chauncey."

"Hi, Chauncey. What is it? You've never called me before. Something wrong?"

"Catherine, it's concerning Tony. I don't know how to tell you this."

"Tell me what, Chauncey?"

"Catherine, Tony was shot. I'm so sorry, Catherine. Tony is gone."

Catherine screams.

The Funeral

It's the day of Tony's funeral. The sky is dark, and the clouds appear heavy with rain. Catherine is dressed in all black with a wide-brimmed black hat that dips low to cover her eyes. Catherine and the children prepare for Chauncey's arrival. He will take them to the homegoing service. Catherine's heart is heavy. The house is quiet. No one speaks as they wait for Chauncey.

Chauncey arrives and knocks on the door. Catherine answers. "Hello, Chauncey."

Chauncey hugs Catherine and tries to comfort her. Yet there is nothing that can comfort Catherine. Catherine and the children leave the house with Chauncey and get into his car.

When they arrive to the church, the rain begins to pour. They rush to get inside before they are drenched. Chauncey leads Catherine to the front of the sanctuary. Everyone at the club recognizes her as the woman Tony was going to marry and embraces her as family.

Guests are allowed viewing of the body before the service begins. Catherine, staff, and close family form a line to see Tony one last time. Once the viewing has ended, a male vocalist begins to sing a song by Nat King Cole, "Unforgettable."

Catherine's tears fall more freely as the lyrics significantly represent her feelings for Tony. Family and friends are touched, but the officiating minister attempts to change the atmosphere from one of pain and loss to one of joy and celebration.

"Family, friends, this is a joyous occasion. We will see Tony again. He's in a better place. I am told he had kind heart and was a great friend to all who knew him. So yes, he's unforgettable. He will always remain in our hearts."

When the minister requests words from close friends or family, Catherine walks to the podium. She leans close to the microphone as she speaks.

"Good morning, friends and family. This is a very sad occasion. One that I—" Before she can complete her sentence, a tear escapes her eye and rolls down her cheek. She attempts to catch her breath, but words fail to escape her lips. Chauncey steps up to assist her. He gently touches her elbow and leads her from the podium back to her seat.

The ceremony is short, and the benediction is heartfelt. Family and friends hug and comfort one another. Pallbearers are requested to carry the body to its final resting place. The minister closes the service and dismisses the guests.

Part II: The 80s

Chapter Nine

Victor's Release

Four years later, Victor is released early on good behavior. He calls his friend Trent.

"Hey. Trent. It's Vic."

"What's up, Vic? I thought you were in the pen."

"I was, but they're releasing me today, man. Can you pick me up?"

"Sure, I got you. What time?"

"Now," Victor laughs.

"I'm on my way."

It takes Trent a little more than an hour to get there. When he arrives, he walks inside the building and asks the guard where prisoners awaiting release are held. The security guard escorts Trent to the waiting room.

"What's up, old friend?" Trent asks upon seeing Victor.

"You, man. It's all about you. Thank you for picking me up."

The two friends drive back to the city.

"Drop me off at Catherine's place, alright?"

"You sure you want to do that? It's been a minute since you've seen her. Might want to change out of that prison garb first."

"Yeah, you're right. Take me home. I'll get with her tomorrow."

The Return

The next day, Victor pulls up at Catherine's home. His hair is trimmed short. He is clean shaven and dressed in suit and tie and wearing patent leather dress shoes. He knocks on Catherine's door.

"Who is it?" Catherine asks.

"Vic."

Catherine is speechless. She didn't know Victor had gotten out of jail. She pauses before she speaks, unsure of how to respond. Through closed door, "What is it, Victor? What do you want?"

"Open the door, Catherine. I want to see you."

"No, Victor. Please go away. I don't want to see you."

"Come on now, baby. Don't be like that. I haven't seen you in four years. Is this the way you treat an old friend?"

"We're not old friends, Vic. Please go home."

"I'm not leaving until you open the door, Catherine. I can stand here and knock all day."

Catherine opens the door.

"Victor, please leave me alone. Our relationship is over. I have moved on with my life. I'm clean now. I've put the past behind me. You are my past."

"Oh, is that what I am?" Victor tries to reach for her, but she pushes him away.

"Please go away, and don't ever back here again," Catherine says.

"Alright, I'll leave for now, Catherine, but I'll be back. You can count on that."

Catherine closes the door, places her head in her hands and wonders, *Now what am I going to do?* She picks up the telephone and calls Felicia.

"Hello?" Felicia asks.

"Hi, Felicia. It's Catherine."

"Hi, my friend. How are you?"

"Not good. Guess who just showed up at my door?"

"Who?"

"Victor."

"Oh no. Is he still there? Did he leave?"

"Yes, he's gone, but he said he's coming back."

"I don't know what to do."

"Call the police."

"And say what? He hasn't done anything, and I don't really know if I want the police at my door again. The last time I saw the police, they were taking my children away."

"Yes, I know. What are you going to do?"

"I don't know yet. I just don't know."

The Deal

Meanwhile, Victor is at home, trying to figure out how to come up with some quick cash. He has lost connection with most of his runners while in prison. He dials phone number after phone number, hoping one of his former runners will answer. He has to figure out a way to get back on his feet, and he needs to figure it out fast. Finally, someone answers his call.

"Hello?"

"Darnell, it's Vic. Man, where are all my boys?"

"Hey Vic. You out?"

"Yes, just got out yesterday."

"Okay, cool. You know everybody kind of split up after you went to prison, man. Most of them are running for other people now. Personally, I just got myself a little job working at the car wash. I moved back in with my mom, and I'm trying to make that work."

"You know that car wash can't pay you like I paid you. You want to make some real cash, meet me at my house in about an hour."

"Okay, I'll be there."

An Hour Later

Darnell has taken the bus to Victor's house. He gets off at the bus stop and walks the rest of the way on foot. When he arrives, he knocks on the door. Victor opens it.

"I was expecting you. Glad you came. Come in and have a seat."

Darnell takes a seat on one of Victor's bar stools.

"So what's up, Vic? How are you?"

"I'm good. Listen, this is what I need you to do. I saved a thousand dollars in a cash box and hid it before I was arrested. Thank goodness it's still where I left it. However, I need to flip this thousand into five thousand, you know, how we do. Can I count on you?"

"What's my percentage?"

"Ten percent, same as always."

"Vic, it's just you and me now. It's not like you have to split it with other runners. I'm all you got. I know you can do more than that. What's up?"

"Oh, you've gotten smarter since I've been gone. Alright, alright. Twenty-five percent. That's my final offer, and don't blow this because you know I don't play."

"I got you, Vic. It's a deal. You can count on me."

"Alright, good. Go do what you do and bring back my five gs. I know you can do it."

"Bet."

Darnell calls his contact and sets up the deal.

In less than two weeks, he has the money and returns to Victor's house. Victor opens the door. "Alright, give me the good news."

"I told you I got you, man." Darnell hands him $5,000, and Victor gives Darnell twenty-five percent.

"Okay, now let's flip one more time," Victor says.

"No problem."

"Alright, now I need to go see my old lady and let her know I'm back on my feet." Victor laughs.

Victor drives to Catherine's house. He doesn't see the car following him. As he pulls up to Catherine's home and gets out of the car, two men jump out of their car and rush him. They grab him and hit him several times in the face and stomach. Victor yells.

Catherine hears yelling and loud thuds against her front porch. She peeks out the window. She observes two men roughing up Victor. She reluctantly calls the police, knowing this incident could jeopardize her maintaining custody of her children.

With sirens blaring, the police arrive and find Victor bloodied and beaten. The two men who had jumped him ran when they heard the sirens.

The police call for an ambulance and begin to question Catherine.

"Ma'am, do you know what happened here?"

"No sir," Catherine replies. "I just heard a lot of noise, and when I looked out of my window, I saw people fighting in front of my house, so I called the police."

"Understood. Well, we'll need to get a statement from you in the morning. Can you come to the station?"

"Sure," Catherine says. "No problem."

The ambulance arrives, and Victor is taken to the hospital. After everyone leaves, Catherine returns to her house. She walks inside, locks the door, and sits on the sofa. She realizes the gravity of her situation. She decides she will not go into the station to make a statement the next day. She never wants to see Ms. Saunders back at her door again conducting any type of investigation. More important, she doesn't want to be there if the men who beat up Victor return. Therefore, she feels her only option is to leave. She must get as far away from Victor and the company he keeps as she possibly can. She must protect her children.

The Note

Later that night, Catherine writes a note to her children: "My dear children. Words cannot express the love I have for you and for your overall protection. There is a situation that has caught up with me, and I cannot jeopardize your life or your safety. Please go to your grandmother's house and stay there until arrangements have been made for us to be together again. Please do not look for me or try to find me. This is for your own safety. I love you very much."

The Next Day

Tina awakes first as she normally does. It's 9:00 a.m., and her stomach is growling. Normally, her mother would be up by now cooking breakfast, but she doesn't smell anything cooking. The house is quiet. *Maybe Mom's still asleep.* She decides to check. She looks in her mother's bedroom; the bed is made as if she hasn't slept in it all night. She wakes up Leon.

"Leon, have you seen Momma?"

Leon rubs his eyes and stretches. "Not since last night. What's up?"

"She isn't here."

"Maybe she left a note like she did last time. Check the fridge."

Tina finds the note taped to the refrigerator, reads it, and returns to Leon's room in tears.

"What's wrong, Tina?"

"Read this, Leon."

Leon reads the note and calls his grandmother.

"Hello?"

"Hi, Grandma. It's Leon."

"Good morning, Leon. Do you know it's just nine? Why are you calling so early on the weekend?"

"Momma's gone, Grandma. She left a note. She doesn't want us to look for her or try to find her. She said it's for our own safety. The note also says she wants us to move in with you until we can be together again."

"Jesus. What's going on? I'm worried for her and for the three of you. I don't know what's going to happen now."

"Neither do we, Grandma. Can we pack and move in with you like she said?"

"Leon, you know I love you all very much, but I can't afford to care for you. I wish I could. I really do. I just don't have the money. What's the name of that caseworker who was involved with your case a few years ago?"

"Ms. Saunders, but Grandma, Tina and I are grown now. I'm nineteen, and Tina's twenty. We can't go to foster care."

"That's true, but Michelle is only fifteen. She's considered a minor. I'll have to call Ms. Saunders for her."

"Couldn't we petition the court and take care of her ourselves, Grandma? Maybe Tina and I could find a place and take her with us."

"Yes, but that process takes time, Leon. In the meantime, we must call Ms. Saunders first thing Monday morning."

"Alright. I need to wake up Michelle. This is going to break her heart. But what else can we do?"

"I know, baby. I know, and I'm so sorry. I wish I could take all three of you. Really I do. For now, you and Tina can stay with me until you find a place of your own, and Michelle can stay until Ms. Saunders makes arrangements to pick her up. Oh, and please make sure you write down the number for Ms. Saunders for me."

"Alright. Thanks, grandma. We'll be there in an hour."

Leon walks to Michelle's room and knocks on the door. No answer. He knocks again. "Michelle, get up. I need to talk to you."

Michelle gets out of bed and opens the bedroom door. "Leon, I'm trying to sleep. It's the weekend. What are you waking me up for?"

Leon tries to break the news to Michelle as gently as he can.

"No. Where's Momma? Where is she? I won't go back to foster care. Please! I can't." Michelle sobs.

"It's going to be okay, Michelle. Don't cry."

In light of the safety issue, Tina decides not to cook breakfast. They eat a quick bowl of cereal, lock the door, and head to the bus stop. They arrive at their grandmother's house shortly thereafter. Leon knocks on the door.

"Who is it?"

"Leon, Tina, and Michelle."

Grace opens the door. "Come on in. Let me show you to your rooms. Leon, you'll have to sleep in your Uncle Phil's room, and Tina and Michelle will have to share a room with Stacy. It's going to be crowded for a minute. But let's try to make it work for now."

"Alright, thanks Grandma," Leon says.

"Yes, thank you," Tina says.

Michelle is silent.

Later that evening, Grace calls the children for dinner. "Okay everyone, dinner's ready. Wash your hands and come to the table."

Everyone appears except Michelle.

"Where's Michelle?" Grace asks.

"Maybe she's still lying down in Stacy's room. I'll get her," Leon says.

Leon looks for Michelle in Stacy's room but doesn't find her. He knocks on the bathroom door, but she is not there either. He searches the entire house, calling her name. There is no answer. By now, everyone else in the house is looking as well. Stacy and Tina were yelling, "Michelle, where are you?"

In fear of returning to foster care, Michelle has run away.

Chapter Ten

The Runaway

Michelle runs as fast as she can. She doesn't want Tina, Leon, or anyone to find her. When she has turned enough corners to ensure she is out of sight, she stops to catch her breath. She looked across the street at a playground, where she goes and sits on a bench. She begins to contemplate if life is worth living.

Considering that her mom has left, her brother and sister are grown and can go wherever they want, and she is at the mercy of foster parents and whatever abuse they might inflict, Michelle thinks, *I should just end it all right now.*

She searches through her backpack for her pencil sharpener, remembering the small blade inside it. She can't find it. As she ponders where it might be, she remembers the youth home and some of the children who were with her prior to her foster care placement with the Johnsons. She remembers Cedric and how nice he had treated her. She hopes she still had his number. Searching through her backpack once more, she finds her phone book and flips through its pages. "Yes, here it is. Now to find a telephone booth."

Michelle walked a few more blocks until she spots a phone booth. She rushes to it and puts a quarter in the slot. She dials Cedric's number.

"Hello?"

"May I speak with Cedric?"

"This is he."

"Hi, Cedric. This is Michelle. I know it's been over four years since I've last spoken with you, but I remember how kind you were and was hoping you could help me."

"Sure, Michelle. Yes, of course I remember you. What's up?"

"I need a place to stay. It's only temporary, until I can find a job. I promise I won't stay long. Please! I'm in trouble."

"Well, I guess it will be okay, temporarily. But I live in a studio apartment, and I have only one room and one bed."

"That's fine. I can sleep on the floor."

"Alright. Well, do you have a pencil?"

"Yes."

"Here's my address."

Cedric provided Michelle with his address. She found a bus stop and waited fifteen minutes before a bus arrived. She got on and requested a transfer since she would need to catch an additional bus to get to Cedric's apartment.

The Apartment

She rings the doorbell to his studio apartment. She looks at her watch. It is after 8:00 p.m. Cedric asks through the intercom, "Who is it?"

Michelle presses the intercom button. "It's Michelle."

Cedric buzzes her in.

Michelle enters Cedric's apartment.

"Hi, Cedric. Thank you so much for helping me."

"No problem, Michelle. Where are you bags?"

"I only have my backpack and whatever I could stuff into it."

"Ah, man that's tight. You *are* in trouble."

"I just need a job. I'll be okay."

"Alright, are you hungry?"

"Yes."

"Okay, you can fix yourself something to eat. There are blankets in the linen closet. I need to go to work. I'll see you later, okay?"

"Okay. Thank you, Cedric."

"You're welcome."

Cedric works the night shift, from 9:00 p.m. to 3:00 a.m., at a bottling factory. Although it is assembly line work he doesn't like, it pays the bills. He has a run-down car, but it gets him where he needs to go. He starts the engine. It putts for a few seconds before starting up.

At 3:35 a.m., Cedric returns to his studio apartment. He comes in quietly. It's dark, but he can see by moonlight Michelle's outline on the floor. Cedric lies down beside her and slips under the blankets. He begins to touch and fondle Michelle. Michelle wakes. Realizing what is happening, she jumps up.

"What are you doing?"

"You need a place to stay, right?"

"Yes, and—"

"You need food, apparently clothing too, right?"

"What are you getting at, Cedric?"

"Well, I have needs too."

"Please, Cedric. I can repay you a different way. Let me get a job. I'll pay you. I promise."

"Oh I know you will, but tonight you're mine."

The next morning, Michelle tiptoes through the apartment, hoping desperately not to awaken Cedric. She slowly opens the door and quietly closes it behind her. As she walks to the bus stop, she realized she has made a mistake running away.

After getting on the bus, she rings the bell upon sight of the first telephone booth. Tears well up in her eyes. She dials her grandmother.

"Hello?"

"Hello, Grandma. This is Michelle."

"Michelle, where are you? We were worried sick about you!"

"Grandma, I'm sorry. Can someone come get me? I didn't have enough money for a transfer."

"Tell me where you are and I'll have your Uncle Phil pick you up."

Michelle provides Grace with her location.

Grace hangs up and calls out, "Tina?"

"Yes, Grandma?"

"Go get your Uncle Phil. Michelle just called, and Phil needs to pick her up immediately."

"Thank God. Okay, I'll get him now," Tina says.

Phil picks up Michelle and returns to Grace's house. Michelle is quiet, and Phil does not pry. When Michelle walks in, everyone is happy to see her, but Michelle begins to cry.

The Deception

Michelle decides not to tell anyone what happened. She pretends she is crying only because of her fear of returning to foster care. No one suspects anything different.

On Monday morning, Grace calls Ms. Saunders and explains the chain of events leading to the children staying with her. Ms. Saunders makes arrangements to return Michelle to the youth group home by the end of the week.

That Friday, Ms. Saunders picks up Michelle, and everyone hugs and kisses Michelle good-bye. Tina cries, and Leon tries to console them.

"Don't worry, Michelle. Tina and I are going to petition the court to get custody of you. Don't worry. I love you, and we'll see you again soon."

Ms. Saunders drives Michelle to the youth group home. Upon arrival, Ms. Dayton opens the door.

"Welcome back, Michelle. Good to see you."

"Hi, Ms. Dayton. Please show me my room."

"Right this way, young lady."

Six Weeks Later

Michelle awakes at 6:00 a.m. and runs to the bathroom. She gags and throws up in the toilet.

"What's wrong, child? Are you ill?" Ms. Dayton asks.

"I need to go to the doctor."

Ms. Dayton schedules an appointment for two weeks from that day. Michelle is examined by a doctor. Blood work is administered as well. Michelle is seven weeks pregnant.

Foster Home Number Two

The telephone at the group home rings. Ms. Dayton picks up the handset.

"Hello?"

"Good morning, Ms. Dayton. This is Ms. Saunders."

"How are you, Ms. Saunders?"

"I'm fine, and I have great news to share with you and Michelle."

"Really? What is it?"

"We've found a placement for Michelle."

"That's great, but there's something you need to know."

"What's that?"

"Michelle's pregnant."

"Oh my. Well, let's not tell Michelle just yet. I need to make sure the foster home is licensed for teenage mothers as well. I believe they are, but I need to make certain."

"Okay. Just call me back when you find out."

"Wait a minute. Ms. Harvard, the foster parent, may be at home. Can you hold for a moment while I call her?"

"Yes."

Ms. Saunders places Ms. Dayton on hold and dials Ms. Harvard.

"Hello?"

"Hello, may I speak with Ms. Harvard?"

"This is she."

"Ms. Harvard, this is Ms. Saunders, the caseworker."

"Oh, yes. Hi, Ms. Saunders. How are you?"

"I'm fine. However, we have new developments with the case of Michelle Hilton."

"What's going on?"

"I've just found out Michelle is pregnant. I can't remember off the top of my head, but aren't you licensed for teenage mothers as well?"

"Yes I am."

"Great, then may we proceed with the placement?"

"Yes ma'am."

"Alright, I'll inform Ms. Dayton, the youth home director, and we'll see you next week."

One Week Later

Ms. Saunders arrives at the home of Ms. Lillie Harvard, Michelle's new foster care mother. Michelle walks to the door. She is nervous, pregnant, and afraid. Ms. Saunders rings the doorbell. Ms. Harvard peers through the peephole, recognizes Ms. Saunders, and opens the door.

"Good morning Ms. Saunders, and hello, who do we have here?"

"Hi, Ms. Harvard. This is Michelle. Michelle, this is Ms. Harvard."

"Hi Michelle," Ms. Harvard says. "I've been waiting for you."

"Waiting for me?" Michelle looks puzzled. "Really?"

"Yes, it's a long story, but come on in. We have all the time in the world."

"Michelle, you go on in, and I'll get your suitcase out of the car. I don't want you carrying anything heavy in your condition."

"Thank you, Ms. Saunders."

"Please have a seat Michelle," Ms. Harvard says as she points to the sofa.

Ms. Saunders returns with her suitcase and sets it in the living room.

"Well, I guess I'll be leaving now," Ms. Saunders says.

"Alright. Thank you, Ms. Saunders, and have a nice day," Ms. Harvard says.

"Good-bye, Ms. Saunders," Michelle says. She blinks and quickly brushes away a tear. Ms. Harvard pretends not to notice.

"You'll be fine, Michelle. I'll be in touch and check on you from time to time, okay?"

"Okay."

Ms. Saunders leaves.

"Well, I have a story to tell you," Ms. Harvard says.

"A story? What kind of story?"

"You see, you're not going to believe this, but I had a dream about a young teenage mother coming to live with me. In this dream, we were very close, and nothing could separate us because of the love God Himself placed in our hearts for one another as mother and daughter.

Now I know you may think, 'What's this lady talking about?' but I know that child is you."

"How do you know for sure?" Michelle asks.

"Michelle, God placed you here because He wants you to know your pain is over. He has heard your cry, and He has sent a comforter, for He loves you and He cares for you. He desires for you to be happy and whole. You are precious in His sight. Your struggle is over. Welcome home, Michelle. Welcome home."

Michelle smiles. Somehow, she can sense something different about this woman, something honest and sincere. She knows she will be okay.

About the Author

Lorna Jackie Wilson was born in Detroit on April 11, 1964, to Carrie Jean Wilson. At age four, she was placed in foster care. Reflections of her childhood with her mother and siblings draw memories of fishnets hung from the ceiling with Polaroid photos hanging in the balance as the record player's needle dropped to spin songs such as "Me and Mrs. Jones" and "Lost in a Masquerade."

Most of her childhood memories are fond, as she eagerly anticipated each day playing outside with her siblings. During the 1970s, she and her siblings were rarely inside. They played outdoors daily as they engaged in traditional games such as jump rope, hopscotch, and basketball. In fact, they usually played outdoors until the street lights came on. Little did they know that their mother had an addiction to controlled substances.

Consequently, when foster care came to take her and her siblings away, she was distraught and torn. At age ten, she was returned to her mother, and she and her siblings were reunited only to be separated again when she was thirteen. In all, Lorna was in and out of foster care for eleven years. While the journey reveals a combination of pain and loss, it also reveals love, laughter, and accomplishment.

The last foster home Lorna entered was while she was pregnant with her first child. Acie Spraddling is the foster mother who introduced her to Father God and His precious Son, Jesus Christ. Acie led by example. This is where Lorna's singing and writing began.

In 2013, Lorna earned a trophy as one of the finalists in a national singing competition sponsored by William Beaumont Hospital in Royal Oak, Michigan.

Finalists created a CD at Advanced Recording Studios and were entered into a casting and talent booking network, the American Performing Arts Network.

Lorna is the mother of four beautiful children, all of whom support her work in literary art and music.

In 2005, Lorna earned a bachelor's degree in business administration. In 2007, she earned a master's degree in business education, and in 2012, she earned a second master's in information technology.

Lorna is also a member of Detroit World Outreach, her church home where an awesome worship experience takes place under the leadership of Bishop Ben and Dr. Charisse Gibert.

Bibliography

Answers (2014). "Meaning and Origin of Matthew Surname." Retrieved from http://genealogy.answers.com/last-names/meaning-and-origin-of-matthew-surname.

Pecora, P., et al. (2003). "The Foster Care Alumni Studies, Stories from the Past to Shape the Futures." Addressing the Effects of Foster Care: Early Results from the Casey National Alumni Study (Seattle, Washington).

About the Book

Eleven-year-old Michelle and her siblings live in an urban area with their mother, Catherine, until the day they are separated and placed in different foster homes due to circumstances beyond their control. Their journeys take them in directions that question and challenge their lifestyles and senses of identity while significantly impacting their self-esteem, purpose, and well-being.

Printed in the United States
by Baker & Taylor Publisher Services